PHOENIX

JACQUELIN THOMAS

Phoenix © 2019 by Jacquelin Thomas

ISBN: 978-1699521250 (Print)

Photo Credit:
Rebecca Pau (www.thefinalwrap.com)

For every minute you are angry you lose sixty seconds of happiness.

~Ralph Waldo Emerson

Chapter One

"WDNC News reporter Cynthia Highcloud suffered life-threatening injuries eight weeks ago when an unidentified SUV slammed into the vehicle she was driving, forcing her car off the road and flipping twice. Anyone who might have information is asked to contact police at 214-555-3621."

"Turn it off." Her words floated on the moan that escaped her lips.

A nurse dressed in royal blue scrubs entered the room. "Miss Highcloud... the police are here. They want to talk to you."

She released a heavy sigh, despite the pain that came with it. "Send them in," Cynthia managed after a moment.

When she first woke to an awareness that she was in a hospital, Cynthia had no idea how she'd ended up there. She'd gone into a panic when she realized her jaw had been wired shut to the point she had to be sedated. She was twenty-eight years old and had never once fractured or broken any parts of her body. Cynthia had been pretty healthy most of her life.

Later with her parents by her side, Cynthia was informed by her doctor that her first surgery had taken four and a half hours to stabilize the fractures in her jaw and face. He also explained that she would have to undergo a second surgery to repair the damaged facial features and restore functioning.

It wasn't until the fourth or fifth day after the incident that Cynthia began to remember some of the details of what happened. Detectives had come by the hospital to interview her, but the questions only frustrated her to the point of tears and a rise in her blood pressure. They were advised to wait until she was much stronger.

She did give them a note which said: *someone tried to kill me.*

The wiring in her mouth was removed a couple of days ago.

Cynthia had her father call the detectives. She was ready to talk.

The two men dressed in dark suits entered the sterile-looking hospital room.

"Miss Highcloud, I'm Detective John Harlow and this is my partner Simon Geoff. We came to speak with you before—"

"I remember," she said.

"How are you feeling?"

She did not respond, just gestured toward the bandages covering her face. After a moment, Cynthia spoke again. "This wasn't some random accident. That car was following me."

"Do you know this for sure?" Geoff asked.

She gave a slight nod, sending a sharp knifelike pain through her body. "I noticed it the moment I left the station, but at the time, I didn't think anything of it. Then every turn I made; I noticed the car stayed behind me—I couldn't see who was driving, the car was a Mercedes. I'm sure of that. When I exited the freeway, the driver grew bolder. I was afraid so I sped up and now... I'm here in the hospital with my face so messed up, I barely recognize myself."

John Harlow had kind eyes. Cynthia estimated that he was in his late thirties; he was African American with a thin wisp of a mustache and close-cropped hair. He had a robust face that probably lit up when he laughed, and brown eyes tinged with a certain sternness, yet his genuine concern for her came through.

"Can you think of anyone who might have wanted to harm you?"

"I investigate high profile people. Some of them don't like me very much, but to try and kill me... I don't know."

Simon Geoff was the taller of the two. He looked to be senior detective in years and experience. "We're going to find the person responsible, Miss Highcloud. Where you en route to anywhere in particular that night?"

I live in Willowbend. I was on my way home." Cynthia attempted to sit up in bed but found the act too painful. "I recently did an expose' on Abraham McCormick. He drugged and raped several women when he was in college."

Geoff handed her the control to raise up the head of her bed, then asked, "You mean Pastor McCormick? McCormick Ministries?"

"Yes."

"It's worth checking out," Detective Harlow said. "I followed that story. Five women have come forth, accusing this man of drugging and raping them."

"I received threats after I exposed McCormick. I saved the emails. They came from an anonymous account."

"We need to see them," Geoff said.

"I can have someone from the station forward them to you," Cynthia responded. She made a mental note to give her co-worker the password when she stopped by later this afternoon.

She lay back, feeling exhausted by the mere act of talking.

"We don't want to tire you out, Miss Highcloud. This is all we need from you right now," Geoff stated.

"I'll leave my card on this table. If you think of anything, please do not hesitate to call," Harlow said. "We are hoping for a speedy recovery."

"Please stop McCormick before he hurts someone else."

The May sunshine forced it way into her hospital room, warming her with its rays. Spring was her favorite season until tragedy struck—it would always be remembered as a time of stark fear and facing what she thought was her impending death.

Pain stabbed at her from head to toe. She gulped hard, hot tears slipping down her cheeks.

Fingers trembling, Cynthia pressed the call button.

"What can I do for you, Miss Highcloud?"

"I need more pain meds p-please."

"I'll be right there."

She moaned as another wave of agony flowed through her body.

━━━

"YOU'RE NOTHING BUT A CRIMINAL, Abraham McCormick."

His expression was a mask of stone. "Brother Thomlinson... if you'd just let me explain—"

"You can't explain this away," he interjected. "What you did to those women is reprehensible. Then to find out you propositioned my daughter when she ran into you at the mall." Bud Thomlinson was beet red in the face and his eyes bulged more than normal in his fury.

"I did no such thing," Abraham stated. "If I want new clothes—I see my tailor and he isn't located at the mall." He had no idea why Thomlinson's daughter would lie on him like that.

"Sarah Anne wouldn't make up something like this. I hope they lock you up and throw away the key."

"Bud Thomlinson, you have two-seconds to leave my husband's office before I call security," Sophia stated from the doorway. "Not only is Sarah Anne lying on Abraham—she smokes marijuana and who knows what else she's doing. Maybe you need to keep a closer eye on your daughter."

Bud's face was marked by loathing. "You're no better than your husband."

"Leave my wife out of this," Abraham demanded. "You've had your say... now leave..." He'd had enough of Bud's threats and menacing behavior. Abraham wasn't about to allow the man behave in the same manner toward Sophia.

"I'm gonna see that you pay for what you did," He uttered before storming out of Abraham's office.

Closing the door, Sophia said, "Bud makes what? The seventh or eighth person who's come in here to threaten you this morning."

"They're angry," Abraham responded. "Since those women came out of nowhere with their lies--everyone seems to want to believe the worse of me. Those women lying like that... When Bud's family needed help with their mortgage, we came to their rescue. When the Morton's couldn't bury their son—we took care of everything. Now these same people are in an uproar. I don't understand how they can so easily believe a lie."

"Two of the women that started these lies—y'all went to the same college. Are you sure you don't remember them? It was only ten years ago."

Abraham shook his head. "No. Something may have happened to them in school, but I didn't do it."

He walked over to the window, staring out. "I don't understand why someone is targeting me like this."

"We just moved into our new church. Your ratings on television are exploding. The growth in members has been phenomenal—maybe one of the other pastors in the area feels threatened and is behind this smear campaign to ruin your reputation."

Abraham turned to face his wife. "But to have a bunch of women come forward to accuse me of attacking them? I don't remember ever meeting any of those women, including Adrienne. And I certainly didn't try to seduce Sarah Anne."

"Don't nobody want that frog-faced girl," Sophia uttered. "Her eyes are way too big for that head of hers."

He broke into a tiny smile. "Sweetheart…"

"You know I'm telling the truth."

Abraham changed the subject by asking, "Have you heard anything about that reporter's condition? She was on my mind this morning when I woke up."

Sophia met his gaze. "I thought I was the first thing on your mind, husband." She opened the lightweight coat to reveal her physical attributes. The matching purple dress fit her body like a glove.

Abraham openly admired her curves, pausing briefly on

her full and firm bosom. "Honey... you know you're the one who owns my heart." She was not only beautiful, but also a brilliant businesswoman. At thirty-three years old, Sophia was slender and long-limbed with an abundance of shoulder-length jet curls; black opal eyes; full, sensual lips; and deep mocha skin.

"After what that woman did to you—I wouldn't waste a moment thinking about her. I'm not saying she deserved what happened, but I guess Cynthia Highcloud angered one person too many." Sophia glanced down at her nails and frowned. "I need a manicure in the worst way."

"I have a meeting with my attorney at eleven. Are you going with me?"

Sophia shook her head. "No. It's too much for me to deal with, Abraham. I've never been so humiliated. Members are leaving the church in droves and causing scenes. Those tramps and that reporter decided to band together... for *what*? Money? Look where she is now... I'm just saying."

He walked over to his wife and embraced her. "Everything will work out, sweetheart. The truth will come out and I'll be vindicated."

She backed out of his arms. "Abraham, do you hear your-self? Everything is *not* going to be okay. We're going to be bankrupt because of that witch."

Sophia had been asked to resign as chairperson over the Dallas Women's Club because of Cynthia Highcloud. She was no longer one of the most envied women in the city. Instead, she was now the subject of juicy gossip and ugly social media memes. Several of their employees had stabbed them in the back by selling stories to news outlets. Abraham imagined it took every fiber of Sophia's being to walk around with her head held high, pretending as if she had not been tainted by the scandal.

Abraham pulled her into his embrace once more, holding her close. "I'm sorry this is happening, but I promise I'm going to make it up to you."

"And how are you gonna do that?"

"I have no idea at the moment," he confessed. "The first step is proving my innocence."

"There were pictures of you with that Adrienne chick. It was during a time when you were drinking and partying a lot. Maybe you blacked out, Abraham. You used to have them from time to time."

"I would never resort to rape, Sophia. I need you to trust me in this."

"I haven't left you… I have to tell you that they don't make it easy though. This is a lot to deal with. At the time I didn't think it was possible, but we survived the scandal of the breakup of your first marriage. But Abraham, this is so much worse."

He nodded in understanding.

"You may want to have Shadow stationed outside your office," Sophia suggested.

Abraham shrugged in nonchalance. "I don't think that's necessary."

"Did you miss that murderous expression on Bud's face?" She switched her designer purse from one shoulder to the other. "Because I didn't. You know he has a terrible temper."

"I'm not afraid of Thomlinson."

Sophia placed a hand lovingly to his cheek. "Just be careful, Abraham. I can't bear the thought of someone hurting you."

They heard a loud voice outside the office.

"I'm here to see that rapist McCormick and I'm not leaving until I have my say."

Sophia looked at her husband. "You shouldn't have come here. The building's for sale—let Shadow schedule someone to clear out our files. Pretty soon a lynch mob will be coming for you, Abraham. They've already deemed you guilty."

Shadow appeared in the open door. "Dan Roberts is insisting on speaking with you. Do you want me to get rid of him?"

"Yes," Sophia responded.

"No," Abraham said.

Sophia glared at him.

"I'll be fine, sweetheart," he assured her.

"I'm telling you now… if you don't find a way to clear your name, I won't linger around to watch you die. Pay these women off… do whatever you have to do, Abraham."

━━

HE BRISTLED with hatred for Abraham McCormick, a man whose eloquent speaking and sophisticated ways could do nothing for him now. He'd been outed for the fraudulent and perverted pastor that he was, but public humiliation wasn't enough. He wanted him to really suffer.

Honor demanded it.

A drop of sweat rolled down the side of his face as his fingers danced along the cool metal of his weapon as he sat in his car watching as Abraham exited his Mercedes and walked briskly into a house four miles from where he lived.

Not only was he cheating his congregation. He was also cheating on his wife.

A couple of hours passed before Abraham returned to his car.

"It's high time someone put a little scare into you, Pastor McCormick."

He positioned the rifle and fired.

Chapter Two

Cynthia opened her eyes to find her mother seated in a chair positioned next to the hospital bed. Principal Chief Samuel Highcloud and his wife, Tracy left Oklahoma within an hour of receiving word that Cynthia had been in an accident. During the two months she remained hospitalized—they were constant visitors.

"How are you feeling?"

"Mama, I hurt," she whispered. Despite her drug-induced fog to dull her pain; the beeping machines and multiple IV bags, Cynthia took some comfort in her mother's presence.

"Dylan's here, sweetheart. He came straight here from the airport."

Cynthia needed her parents and her fiancé by her side. It really meant a lot to her that Dylan had come home. He was an investigative journalist at a Cairo-based independent newspaper, focusing on environmental and economic issues and political corruption.

Pain ripped through her body as she tried to turn her

head. Her gaze traveled the room, looking for him. "Where is he?"

"Your father took him down to the cafeteria to get something to eat. The nurses told me that Dylan sat in this chair watching you sleep up until we arrived. He had been here since ten this morning."

"What time is it?"

"Twelve-thirty," her mother responded.

"Why didn't he wake me?"

"The doctor says you need to rest as much as possible in order for your body to heal."

"Mama, I'm glad you're here with me," she managed between breaths. "I feel like… it's like I'm either hurting or I feel numb. I'm scared."

Her mother planted a kiss on her hand. "You're safe now."

"It's too dark in here." Tracy got up and walked over to the window to let more of the sunlight inside.

Cynthia's eyes traveled the room. Floral arrangements, balloons, a couple of teddy bears and several cards were stationed all around.

"People from everyone have sent letters. More flowers arrive every day. Your father told them to give us the cards but distribute the arrangements to the terminally ill and children's wing. He figured you'd approve."

"I do," Cynthia said.

"Hey Babe," Dylan greeted as he made his way to the empty chair next to the hospital bed. "Miss Tracy, do you want to sit down? He inquired. "I don't mind standing up."

"I'm actually going to meet Sam downstairs and grab a bite to eat so that you can spend some time alone with Cynthia."

"W-Welcome home," she said when her mother left the room. "I'm just sorry it's under these circu... circumstances."

"I'm so glad you're okay," Dylan said.

"I'm not anywhere n-near being o-okay," Cynthia managed through the pain threatening to resurface with a vengeance. "The doctor said I'm going to need more reconstructive surgery."

Dylan took her hand in his, giving it a light assuring squeeze. "You won't have to do this alone."

"How did you find out about the accident?"

"Your dad called me."

"Dylan, someone tried to kill me. I'm pretty sure it was Abraham McCormick. The car was a Mercedes SUV—the same car he drives."

"Did you tell the police?"

"I did," Cynthia responded. "I told them everything I could remember about that night."

Her parents returned an hour later.

"Nadine called while you were sleeping," her mother announced. "I meant to tell you earlier, but I needed to eat something. She's planning on coming by tomorrow morning to visit you."

"How did she sound?" Cynthia asked. Her friend was one of McCormick's five accusers.

"She sounded really worried about you."

"Nadine needs to be careful," Tracy said. "If what you're saying is true about Abraham McCormick, your friend may be in danger."

Cynthia grew distressed at the thought of Nadine in peril. "Maybe I should have the police check on her." She gestured toward the table. "One of the detective's left his card. Dad,

can you call him. Ask him to please check on the women—
they may all be in trouble."

⊏▭⊐

FRANTIC, Sophia rushed into the emergency room at the
Dallas Memorial Hospital. "I was told that they brought my
husband here," she said. "I need to see him."

One of the nurses escorted her to the back.

"Pastor McCormick is doing fine. The bullet struck him in
the arm. We were able to get it out and clean his wound."

"Thank the Lord," Sophia murmured. She had imagined
a worst-case scenario during the drive there.

She blew through the door like a hurricane. "Abraham..."

"I'm fine, sweetheart," he quickly assured her.

A former nurse, Sophia took a quick assessment of him
and inspected his arm. "Did you have to get stitches."

"Only a couple."

"This has really gotten out of hand," she stated. "Now
someone's shooting at you. This is crazy."

"The Lord was with me. They only got me in the arm. At
least it's not the one I use the most."

"Did you notice anything strange or see anyone?" Sophia
asked.

"No," he responded.

"So, you didn't see the person who shot you?"

"Sweetheart, I already told you that I never saw anyone. I
was on my way home and minding my own business."

Shaking her head, Sophia uttered, "I knew something like
this could happen. You just refused to listen. These so-called
Christians are out for blood. I'd bet money it was Bud Thomlinson who shot at you. He was in the Army, you know."

Abraham considered her words. "I don't know if he'd take it this far, sweetheart. You really think he'd risk going to jail?"

"He probably thinks he's too good to get caught." Sophia sat down in one of the empty chairs. "Where's your car? We're going to have to arrange to get it towed."

"I left it parked on Larsen. After I was shot, I called 9-1-1 and waited for them to arrive. I didn't want to risk passing out while trying to make it home."

"You weren't that far from the house. What I don't understand is how they were able to shoot you while you were driving."

It was obvious, Sophia was determined to get all the details. Abraham decided to be honest. "I wasn't driving. I'd just walked to the car and was about to get in when the shot came out of nowhere."

Sophia frowned. "What were you doing in that neighborhood? It's a residential area. Were you checking on a member of the congregation?"

When he remained silent, her expression changed. "Oh, I understand now. You made a hoe stop."

"Let's not do this here," Abraham said, keeping his voice low.

"Maybe she's the one who shot you. Lord knows I feel like putting a bullet in you right now."

"It wasn't her. I'm positive."

After a moment of tense quietness, he said, "I've been thinking that when this is over, we should leave Dallas. Go somewhere new and start over."

She glanced over at him. "Like where?"

"North Carolina," Abraham said. "It's our home. Once things settle down some, we can start a church there."

"Someone shot at you. We should be making plans to leave

town as soon as we can get our boxes packed. With all this going on, I don't feel safe anymore."

"I can't leave with charges pending against me, sweetheart. But you don't have to stay, Sophia. You can go stay with your mom. See if you can find a place in North Raleigh or Cary."

She sat down on the edge of the hospital bed. "And what if you end up in prison?"

"Sweetheart, I'm not worried about that and you shouldn't either. It's not going to be that easy to get rid of me," Abraham said with a smile. "My attorney will find the truth. We've hired a detective to help out."

"Abraham, you're in serious trouble here. I don't think you're understanding this."

"Those women are lying," he responded. "I'm going to prove it."

She eyed him. "I hope so. I don't like being humiliated like this."

"Sophia, I'm sorry."

She gave a slight shrug. "Unfortunately, it comes with the territory."

"I will make this right."

She eyed the hospital issued gown he wore. "Do you think they're going to keep you overnight?"

Abraham shook his head no. "They're releasing me. I'm waiting on the nurse to come back with the discharge papers any moment now."

"I'm glad you'll be home tonight. I'm really shook up over this."

"Sweetheart, you're safe. I won't let anyone hurt you."

Sophia stood up. "You're the one in the hospital. You need to work on keeping yourself safe before you worry about me."

A nurse entered the room. "I have your discharge paper-work, Pastor McCormick."

He smiled. "Thank you."

Sophia helped Abraham get dressed, then went to get the car.

She met him at the entrance.

Sophia sent Abraham straight to their bedroom as soon as they arrived home from the hospital. "Go on up and get settled. I'll make you a cup of tea. I'd just finished a batch of cookies when the hospital called me."

Sophia's instincts took over when she heard movement behind her in the kitchen. She turned quickly, knife in hand.

"Whoa…"

"*Shadow*…" Sophia uttered, laying the knife on the counter. "You nearly scared the life out of me."

Hands up in the air, he said, "I'm sorry, Mrs. McCormick. I didn't mean to frighten you. Your husband called and asked me to come immediately." His voice was deep and slightly hoarse.

"It's fine. I've been jumpy since Abraham was shot." She put the knife on the counter, then folded her arms across her chest. "I can't believe someone actually tried to kill him. I definitely didn't sign on for something like this."

Her anxiety taking over, Sophia paced, the heels of her shoes clicking a steady rhythm on the hardwood floor. "Someone was angry enough to shoot him. What if they come after me next? Just because I happen to be his wife."

She glanced at Shadow and said, "I'm sorry. I'm just rambling."

When her heartbeat returned to its normal pace, she looked in his direction, mesmerized by his honey brown eyes. She hadn't noticed the golden flecks in his irises in the past.

She decided it was because he kept them hidden behind those dark sunglasses he wore all the time. Sophia took a moment to appreciate his solid muscles and toned body.

Leaning against the counter, Shadow said, "Mrs. McCormick, you don't have to worry. Nothing's gonna happen to you. Not on my watch."

"That gives me some comfort. It's too bad you weren't there with Abraham earlier."

She made one cup of tea and retrieved a second cup from under the espresso machine, placing them both on a tray with the mint chocolate chip cookies she'd made earlier. "Abraham's upstairs resting. The master bedroom is on the left. Take this tray with you when you go up. I remembered how much you enjoy your espresso."

He gave her a rare smile. "Thank you."

Sophia stayed downstairs in the kitchen while Shadow was with her husband. She mixed together the ingredients for peanut butter cookies. She found baking to be relaxing whenever she was anxious.

Her heart nearly skipped a beat when the telephone rang.

Sophia didn't recognize the number on the Caller ID but followed her gut instinct to answer. "Hello."

"Is Abraham McCormick okay?" a feminine voice on the other end asked.

Sophia couldn't believe this bimbo has the nerve to call the house. *Her* house. "Who is this? Why are you asking about *Pastor McCormick?*" she demanded.

"I just want to know that he's okay. He was shot, wasn't he?"

"It wasn't on the news, so how do you know about the shooting?"

Her questions were met with silence.

"You little slut. Don't you ever call my house again unless you're woman enough to take me on." Sophia slammed the phone down.

If Shadow wasn't here, I march right up those stairs and punch Abraham in his arm.

"No wonder you didn't see anyone—you allowed yourself to be distracted. You're so stupid sometimes," Sophia uttered. "I ought to just shoot you myself."

———

"COME IN."

When Shadow entered, Abraham said, "Thanks for coming on such short notice. I told you this morning that I would no longer need your services, but I'm rethinking my decision."

"Did you speak with the police?"

"They don't care what happens to me," Abraham responded, taking the cup of tea from Shadow. "I told them about Bud Thomlinson and his threats, but I doubt they'll even question him. They see me as a villain. My poor Sophia... she doesn't feel safe because of me."

Wincing, Abraham shifted his position. "I think it'd be a good idea for you to stay here in the house."

"You think Thomlinson is stupid enough to do something like this?"

"You saw the way he confronted me at the church after the news report came out? He looked like he wanted to shoot me right there on the spot. I'd like to think he wouldn't, but to be honest... I can't think of anyone else."

"What about Nadine Walters?" Shadow suggested. He

took a sip of the espresso drink. "She goes to a shooting range every weekend."

His body stiffened in shock. "Really? How do you know?"

"I've learned a lot about the ladies who have accused you of rape—it's my job."

"She's lying so why would she go through the trouble of shooting me when it's based on a lie?" Abraham took a sip of tea. "Doesn't make sense to me. Now if it were true—she'd have motive."

"I think she really believes in her lie. That's what makes her dangerous. But regardless, I won't let whoever this person is—he or she won't get that close to you again," Shadow stated.

"Thank you," Abraham murmured. "I've been thinking that I should send Sophia to stay with her mother in North Carolina. Then once I clear my name—I'm going to join her."

"I think it's a good idea," Shadow responded.

"We'd also feel safer if you'd stay here in the house with us for a few days. You can stay in the guest room downstairs."

"I need to go back to my place and pack a few things I'll need while I'm here. I'll be back in a couple of hours."

Abraham nodded. "My pain meds are kicking in. I can barely keep my eyes open."

"Get your rest. I'll take it from here."

"Shadow, I don't know what I'd do without you. Oh, and take the cookies. I have a feeling we're going to be overrun with more. Sophia bakes whenever she's feeling any type of stress."

Chapter Three

Abraham McCormick had been shot.

Cynthia couldn't believe the news, but then again... maybe she could. There were a lot of people upset with him. Although Detective Harlow informed her earlier that Abraham had a solid alibi for the night she was ran off the road—Cynthia wasn't convinced that he didn't have anything to do with her accident.

She blamed him with every fiber of her being and somehow, she would make sure he got what he deserved, time in prison.

Cynthia was in her own version of prison. Every time she looked at this version of her face, she broke down in sobs. She wasn't grateful to be alive. She was angry. Right after the first surgery, Cynthia saw no point in living, but she persevered through a range of surgical and non-invasive techniques by two different plastic surgeons—all in the effort to restore her quality of life and some recognition of self.

The times she gazed at her reconfigured reflection in the

mirror, it was a stranger who stared back. The skin grafts, biocompatible dressings designed to promote healing, and laser treatment to help cover her scars and improve the coloration of her skin. All of this, and the woman she used to be was no more. She had not only changed on the outside, but also on the inside.

"How are you feeling today?" a voice asked from the doorway.

She turned to face her friend, Sabre, but offered no response.

"I know this is not easy for you, Cynthia. I just want you to know that I'm so in awe of you. I'm not sure I could be so strong."

"I know you heard about the shooting."

"I heard," Sabre responded.

"I wish they had killed him."

"Cynthia, you don't mean that."

"Yeah, I do," she countered. "He did this to me. I know it and I'm going to find a way to prove it."

"Why come after you?" Sabre questioned. "You were merely doing your job and reporting the news."

"Those women came to me so I'm sure he probably blames me for everything that happened."

"I know you're very passionate when it comes to issues like this, especially after what happened to Nadine. I wasn't surprised when you decided to take on a man with growing popularity in the Christian community. I'm proud of you, Cynthia. But according to the police, McCormick had nothing to do with your accident."

"He may not have actually committed the crime, but I promise you, Sabre… he's connected in some way. I feel it in my gut."

"Cynthia, what can I do for you?"

"Nothing unfortunately. Not unless you want to take a shot at McCormick for me."

Sabre chuckled. "Naw... I'll pass on that. Nadine is the one who hangs out at the shooting range practically every weekend." She took Cynthia's hand in her own. "If Abraham's responsible, he *will* pay for his crime."

"Not everyone pays for the stuff they do. Gerald Lassiter's a prime example. He raped me and got away with it. No one believed that the star of the football team would do something so vile. Now he's playing in the NFL."

"Gerald's life hasn't been without its drama."

"He deserves whatever he's getting," Cynthia uttered. "I was so excited my freshman year in college. Gerald ruined it for me. I transferred to another school so I wouldn't have to look at his smug face every day."

"I know," Sabre responded. "I still remember that night. You tried to scrub your skin raw and then when I was able to persuade you to come out of the shower—we sat up all night long. I was afraid to close my eyes because I wasn't sure what you might do. You were devastated. I've always blamed myself for what happened to you."

"Sabre, it wasn't your fault."

"Brian and I should've walked you back to the dorm."

"I don't blame you. I'm grateful that when I called you— you came immediately. And you stood by my side even though it cost you your relationship with Brian."

"That jerk..." Sabre uttered.

"The next day, you went with me to report the rape to the campus police. Gerald already had an alibi. There was no evidence..." Cynthia's voice died. "I washed away any traces of him that may have been on my body. I just felt so dirty."

"We were young," Sabre interjected. "We didn't really know any better."

"I thought I'd finally come to terms with what happened in college, but when Nadine reached out to me about McCormick, it was like I was living that nightmare all over again. Nadine is positive that it was Adam McCormick who drugged and raped her last year—she's the reason all these other women came forward."

Cynthia touched the bandage on her face. "Never in a million years did I think that I'd have to live through another horror. Gerald took something from me that I can never get back. Now Abraham McCormick has done the same thing." Her anger had become a scalding fury.

Sabre checked her watch. "I have to get back to the office in about an hour."

"I'll be fine. Dylan's coming by before he has to leave town."

Sabre was clearly not pleased by this. "Okay, I know his work is important, but you need him to be here, Cynthia."

"This isn't easy for him, Sabre. Give him a break."

"It's not easy for *you*. This is the man you're planning to marry in eight months."

Cynthia did not respond.

"You're still getting married, right?"

"I have a lot to deal with, Sabre. Marriage is the last thing on my mind. Besides, Dylan doesn't look at me the same way he used to—I've changed in more ways than one. I'm not the same person."

"You may not look the same, but you're still that same girl I grew up with. Dylan should have the sense to know this." Sabre shook her head in dismay. "If he doesn't, then you should run the other way."

"It's not all him," Cynthia confessed. "A lot has happened. We both need time to process it."

"Hey, you two," Nadine said, entering the hospital room.

She sat down in the empty chair beside Sabre. "You're looking more alert, Cynthia."

"They reduced some of the pain medication." She touched the bandage on her face.

Nadine took her hand. "Don't... you have some of the best doctors in Texas. Everything is gonna be fine."

"She's right," Sabre interjected. "You just focus on letting your body heal. We love you."

"Even if I look like a gorilla?" Nadine chuckled. "Even on your worse day, you could never look like a gorilla. You're a beautiful woman, Cynthia. Your beauty shines from the inside outward. Nobody can take that away from you."

"I know it sounds vain, but I just want to look like me. I don't want to wear someone else's face." Cynthia worried that she would be left with facial scars, the thought sending her into a state of depression.

Nadine looked at Sabre, a confused expression on her face.

"The doctor came in and spread some pictures on the table—he wanted her to pick one," Sabre explained.

"They have to reconstruct my face." She fought back tears. "I don't want a new one. I loved the way I looked."

Nadine took Cynthia's hand in her own. "I had no idea."

"The damage to my face was considerable as Dr. Towson put it." Cynthia's voice broke. "I really could've died in that accident. Sometimes I wish I had instead of going through this."

"We're glad you didn't," Sabre said.

Nadine agreed. "I'm so grateful God spared your life."

"I don't want to look deformed. I know it's selfish of me to say, but it's what I feel."

"I understand, sweetie," Sabre told her. "I just don't think there's any way you'll ever look deformed or hideous, so take that out of your mind. Hey, once I see how you look, I may be giving your doctors a call to have a lil' something done myself, especially to this nose of mine."

Her nurse entered the room. "It's time for your meds, Miss Highcloud. I also need to adjust your IV."

When she left the room, Cynthia told her friend, "Don't even joke about that. Sabre, you have your father's nose. I looked like my mother. Who knows who I'll look like after this?"

"You will always be you," Nadine said.

Her friends stayed with her until she grew tired.

"We'll be back to check on you tomorrow, sweetie," Sabre told her. "I'd come back this evening but Mike's taking me to some fancy dinner."

"And I have to tutor my nephew," Nadine interjected. "He's still struggling with Calculus. I love you, girl."

"Love y'all," she mumbled drowsily.

Cynthia closed her eyes and was soon sleeping soundly, the pain medicine working its magic.

She had been awake for about an hour when Dylan arrived shortly after twelve.

He kissed her gently on the lips. "I would've come earlier, but I had a Skype meeting with my boss."

It was great having Dylan home. His presence always sent her spirits soaring, but this time there was something different about him. It was like he was afraid to get too close.

"When do you have to leave?" Cynthia asked. She knew he had to return to Cairo for work.

"On Friday," he responded. "I really hate leaving you alone to deal with all this."

She shook her head. "Don't worry about it, Dylan. I know that you have a job to do. I understand." Deep down she was anything but happy about his leaving.

"I promise I'll come back as soon as I can, babe."

Cynthia nodded. "I know."

"I still want to marry you."

She smiled. "We'll talk about all that when you come back. Right now, I need to focus on this upcoming surgery."

"Maybe I should take a leave of absence."

Cynthia shook her head no. "My parents will be here with me. I'll be okay."

"I love you."

Cynthia wanted to believe him, but it was difficult to do so when Dylan could barely look her in the face or hide the glimmer of pity that shone in his eyes. After a moment, she responded, "I love you, too."

They talked about his current assignment.

"Sounds like this one could really elevate your career," she said.

"I think so, too."

"Have you given any thought about where you want to have the wedding?" Dylan asked.

"I can't think about that right now," Cynthia responded truthfully.

"We're supposed to get married in about less than a year."

"Dylan, do you see this bandage on my face? Right now, I'm more concerned about how I'm going to look."

"I just thought I'd ask," he stated, rising to his feet. "I'm going to get something to drink. I'll be right back"

"Why are you trying to push that man away?" her mother

inquired when Dylan left the hospital room to grab a cup of coffee. "He loves you."

"He can barely look at me, Mama. And when he does—all I see on his face is pity. Not love and adoration."

"Maybe he just needs some time."

"Mama, we both need that," Cynthia responded, her voice broke miserably. "I need it more than anybody." Changing the subject, she asked, "When will Dad be back?" Her father had to return to Oklahoma last night for work.

"He'll be back Friday night. He pushed back some of his meetings to be here for you. He's done a few Skype meetings —the hospital administrator has been wonderful. She gave him a conference room to use, but he needs to be home to take care of a few things."

He's very dedicated," Cynthia said. Her father was in his first term as the Principal Chief of the Cherokee Nation. Prior to being elected Principal Chief, he served as the Cherokee Nation Secretary of State. He was currently working to establish housing, career training, and building sustainable communities.

Tracy handed her a cup of water with a straw. "Have you thought about what you're going to do once you're able to leave the hospital?"

"I was thinking about coming home for a while," she responded. "After my final surgery."

Her mother released a short sign of relief. "Oh honey... I'm so glad to hear this. I'd be worried if you stayed here in Dallas."

"I told Sabre to put my house on the market. I think it should sell quick."

Her mother agreed. "What will you do with your furniture?"

"I guess I'll just put it in storage for now," Cynthia said. "At this point, I can't really think past my surgery."

"I know this has been very traumatic for you. Your father and I were talking about this earlier. We think you should consider counseling? You've experienced a lot of trauma."

"Dr. Jones suggested it, but I hadn't thought much about it," she answered thickly. The fight for normalcy she once experienced in her life had become a bitter battle. Her thoughts were angry, jagged and painful, leaving her with an inexplicable feeling of emptiness and loss. Cynthia didn't believe a therapist could say anything that would ever make her feel normal again. Her life as she knew it was gone forever.

"THE PHOTOGRAPH of you isn't a fake," Abraham's attorney announced. "It's as real as you and I."

"Okay, so I took a picture with Adrienne, Robert. Doesn't mean I attacked her."

"I have to tell you that it doesn't look good. Adrienne Davis swears that she was at Cody's Pub celebrating St. Patrick's Day. You bought her a couple of drinks before the two of you found a table. She—"

"Wait... St. Patrick's Day," Abraham interrupted. "She's saying I attacked her *that night*?"

"Yes."

"Robert, I wasn't in town. My grandmother's funeral was earlier that day. I was in North Carolina. That photo had to be taken before or after that day, but as for drugging and raping Adrienne—it wasn't me." Abraham felt a sprig of hope. He knew he was innocent—now everyone would know the truth. "I still have the program from her homegoing services. I didn't return to school until the following Monday. I got in late the night before."

He picked up a photo album from under the coffee table and opened it. "Here is a copy of the program for her funeral." Abraham handed a piece of paper to Robert.

"Can I take this?"

Abraham nodded. "I have more copies."

"Do you happen to have an alibi for the date you allegedly attacked Nadine Walters?"

"I've never seen or heard of that woman. She's the one who started this mess." Abraham shook his head. "I'm going to prove that she's nothing but a liar. I don't have to drug women for sex," he uttered. "Did you happen to check to see where she was the night I was shot? I hear she likes to shoot. She's at the DFW Gun Range on the weekends."

"According to the police statement, Miss Walters was at home," Robert stated.

"And they're just going to accept that?" Abraham shook his head. He settled back in the chair disappointed. "They want to believe the worst of me, but these women—they can lie and get away with it."

"Let's take this one step at a time, Abraham." Holding up the program, Robert said, "This is a major victory."

"You look pleased," Sophia stated after Abraham escorted his attorney to the door. "Did Robert give you some good news? If so, you need to share. I've had enough bad news to last me a lifetime."

"Adrienne Davis claimed that I attacked her on St. Patrick's Day."

"*Okaay?*"

"Sweetheart, I wasn't on campus on that day or that

week," he explained. "I was in North Carolina for my grand-mother's funeral."

"But the picture…"

He shrugged in nonchalance. "All I can say is that it couldn't have been taken that day, Sophia. The truth is that I don't even remember meeting that woman."

"So, what about the Denise woman? And that Nadine Walters? Are you able to discredit them as well? I don't think you really have to worry about the others—they don't even look credible. They're definitely not your type."

"We're working on it," Abraham responded. "I just need to prove my innocence."

Sophia wrapped her arms around him. "You don't have to prove anything to me, my love."

"Thank you for believing in me."

"I've known you a long time, Abraham. You would never harm another person unless it was in self-defense."

"The police almost had me questioning myself, especially when they showed me the photo of me and Adrienne. I'm still trying to figure out when and where I met her."

"It was probably at some random party."

"It was right before I met Kendra because that's when I stopped drinking,"

Abraham stated.

"I've always wanted to know what you ever saw in Kendra?" Sophia asked. "She was nice and all, but she didn't look your type. I couldn't believe you married her."

"She believed that there was good in everyone," Abraham said. "Look how she embraced you. She welcomed you into our home because we went to school together. Kendra befriended you and then we betrayed her." A heaviness centered in his chest. He was not proud of his behavior.

"It's her fault for not being woman enough to fight for you. She basically handed you over to me."

Sophia's attitude toward Kendra irked Abraham but he held his tongue. He didn't blame his ex-wife for divorcing him when she discovered his affair. It had gotten around the small town they lived in, which shamed and humiliated Kendra. Abraham acknowledged he would've done the same thing if their roles had been reversed.

"I've never met a pastor's wife who looked so—"

Abraham interrupted her by saying, "That's enough about Kendra. You and I wronged her, Sophia. Let's leave it at that."

━━

CYNTHIA FELT a wave of anger course through her veins when she heard the news. Adrienne Davis' charges against Abraham were dropped. He had a solid alibi once again. It was crazy—

Abraham was one lucky man or so it seemed. He always seemed to be two steps ahead of everyone.

"One day your luck's going to run out," she whispered. It was a shame that Adrienne had gotten the date wrong and had given up so easily.

Her phone rang.

"Nadine, I was just about to call you."

"I just spoke to Adrienne. She's decided not to move forward."

"I heard. Abraham had an alibi for the night she claimed he attacked her," Cynthia stated. "She got the date wrong, so I don't get why she's giving up."

"How is he able to just keep getting away like this?" Nadine wanted to know.

Cynthia hadn't missed the strained tone of her friend's voice. She tried to swallow the lump that lingered in her own throat. "I don't know, but I promise you that I'm going to find out."

"Do you really think he's responsible for what happened to you?"

"Yeah, I do."

"Should I be worried?" Nadine asked. "Do you think he'll come after me?"

Cynthia heard the fear in her friend's voice and felt an instant's squeezing hurt. "I don't know. Just be aware of your surroundings at all times. If you feel like you're being followed —drive straight to the nearest police department."

"I've been staying with my brother," Nadine said. "I also keep my gun with me at all times. I'm not afraid to use it if I have to—I'll shoot on sight."

"I pray it doesn't come to that," Cynthia responded.

Chapter Four

A week later, two more of Abraham's accusers recanted their stories after undergoing thorough and exhaustive interviews.

After he hung up with his attorney, Abraham couldn't wait to call Sophia to tell her the news. "Sweetheart, the one named Denise changed her story. During the interview with the detectives, she actually broke down and confessed that she made it up. The other one, Scarlett... Starlett or whatever she's calling herself—it turns out that she couldn't keep her story straight."

"Are you serious?" Sophia burst into laughter. "I'm not surprised about Scarlett, but Denise... I mean, I knew she was lying but she seemed more credible than Junie."

"Turns out Denise and Adrienne are good friends. I don't know how they thought the police wouldn't find out about their relationship."

"So, the heifer cosigned on a lie."

"I'm just glad the truth is coming out," Abraham said. He felt vindicated but it had come at a huge cost to his career.

"Maybe now, Cynthia Highcloud will come forward and issue a formal apology to you. Our lives are in ruins because of her *investigation*, which as it turns out is sloppy work at best. We should file a lawsuit against her and the TV station."

"Sophia, she's still recovering from that accident. I heard she's had to undergo a couple of surgeries."

"I don't feel bad for her," Sophia uttered. "That's why she's in the situation she's dealing with now. The Lord don't like ugly."

"We should celebrate," Abraham suggested. "Let's go to dinner tonight. You choose the place. I'm leaving the church now."

"I'll be ready."

It didn't take Abraham long to get home, jump in the shower and get dressed.

Humming softly, Sophia seemed happy and relieved that the drama was finally coming to an end.

"You look beautiful," he told her.

She smiled. "Thank you, husband."

In the car, they talked and laughed like a couple on their first date.

A hush fell over the restaurant when they walked in thirty minutes later.

"Everybody's staring at us," Sophia whispered. She felt a shudder of embarrassment.

"Ignore them," Abraham stated.

The manager walked up to them saying, "I'm sorry Pastor McCormick. I don't think it's a good idea for you to dine here tonight. If you like, I can arrange to have your order to go."

"If that rapist is eating here—we're leaving, and we won't patronize this place ever again," a man said loud enough for all of Dallas to hear.

"What is your problem?" Sophia demanded, her humiliation giving way to anger. "For the record, my husband has been cleared of three of the charges. He will soon be cleared of the other two. Those women are nothing but liars."

Turning to Abraham, she said, "Let's get out of here. We don't need to spend money in a place like this."

"Pastor McCormick…" the manager said, "My apologies."

"I don't need your apology," Abraham responded tersely. "We've been loyal patrons of your restaurant for years. This is where we've celebrated birthdays and anniversaries; our church hosted dinners here—we've made you a lot of money and this is how you treat me. I've done nothing wrong."

"Let's go, Abraham," Sophia insisted.

Inside the car, they were silent during the short drive home, each caught up in their own thoughts.

———

"I HAVE NO COMMENT," Cynthia uttered before slamming her phone down. She was tired of reporters calling. She was frustrated with the so-called justice system and how it often failed victims of sexual assault.

She still remembered the rape like it was yesterday. It was her freshman year and she was so excited about being on her own and away from her overprotective parents.

She was taught that no means NO. She knew better than to walk back to her dorm at night alone. But the night Cynthia was raped, she had taken the precaution of being escorted home by someone she knew.

It was the first social event of that academic year at Northeastern State University (NSU) and it had been a fun night. Lectures had not properly begun, and deadlines were still far from everyone's minds. She drank a little, laughed a lot, and danced until she was ready for sleep.

"I think I'm gonna hang out a little longer," Sabre said. "Brian actually wants me to spend the night at his place, so I might not come back to the dorm."

Standing nearby, Gerald Lassiter offered to walk her back to the dorm. "I have to do that way to get to mine."

Cynthia met him her second day on campus through Brian, whom Sabre dated all through high school. He seemed nice enough and walking alone in the dark was something she actively avoided.

"I guess I'll see you in the morning," she told her friend.

On the way to her dorm, they chatted about what to expect with certain professors. Gerald was a sophomore and provided insight on the academic expectations in her classes. There were no red flags.

When they arrived at her dorm, Gerald politely asked if he could come inside. "I think I might have had too much to drink. Do you have coffee?"

"I do," she replied. "C'mon, I make you some."

She never felt unsafe until after he finished drinking the coffee.

The pretense was over.

Cynthia lost count of how many times she said no.

His response, "Why would you let me in if you didn't want something to happen?"

It still astounded her how a charming disguise can so quickly disperse into aggression.

"Gerald, I want you to leave," she told him. "I'm not interested in you like that."

He grabbed her.

Reality set in. Here was someone physically stronger than her, refusing to leave until she gave him what she wanted. Gerald's intentions had never been to get her home safely—this had been his plan all along.

Paralyzed by fear, Cynthia realized that saying no wasn't going to be enough.

When she reported it to the school, Gerald painted her as some drunken female who came on to him and was seeking revenge because he'd rebuffed her. Even with Sabre as a witness to him volunteering to walk her to the dorm did nothing but cause Brian to dump her as his girlfriend.

Gerald's girlfriend lied and said she overheard Cynthia pleading with him to stay with her. She couldn't understand how a woman could cover for a man like that. He ended up marrying her but divorced a year later.

His woes didn't end there, he was now dealing with a second-high profile divorce and he was out for the season with a knee injury. All of which he deserved as far as Cynthia was concerned.

CLENCHING HIS JAW, he released a vicious growl. He punched a hole in the wall, forgetting for the moment that he didn't own the place.

Abraham McCormick had found a way to avoid being charged for sexual assault.

The man was scum. He knew it and couldn't understand why others couldn't seem to see it.

He wasn't worried though.

He would find a way to prove that Abraham was nothing more than a fraud.

Chapter Five

Abraham rubbed his arm. It still throbbed from the bullet wound. "Shadow, after I clear my name, Sophia and I will be moving to Raleigh." They had come to the church to pack up the last of his personal stuff. He couldn't lift anything, so Shadow offered to help, for which he was grateful.

"Really?"

He nodded. "We need a fresh start and I'm pretty sure I won't get one in Dallas. Sophia's already said she no longer feels safe since the shooting. It didn't help being vilified in that restaurant like that—I want to get out of here with my life intact."

Shadow closed up the box he had just packed. "I'd like to join you in North Carolina. You will need security there. We really don't know who made the attempt on your life; so, we have to assume that they will be out there somewhere waiting..."

His words bought a chill to Abraham's body. He could still

feel the way his arm burned as the bullet made its entry and exit.

"I appreciate you wanting to accompany us, but I have to be honest with you. This situation has messed me up financially. I'm going to have to file bankruptcy. Who knows if I'll ever step foot in another pulpit? I'm ruined, Shadow."

"I don't care about the money. I just want to make sure you and your wife are safe. We can figure out the rest later."

"Are you sure about this?"

Shadow nodded. "Where do you want those books?" he asked, pointing to the bookshelf.

"They can go in the box near the door. They should all fit in there."

Abraham sent up a quick prayer of thanksgiving. He hadn't known the man long, but from the moment he entered their lives, Shadow had been a godsend. He was quiet and unassuming, able to blend into any environment, but he was ever vigilant. Abraham trusted Shadow with not only his life but also with his secrets.

"Thank you for everything," he said after all the packing was completed. "I appreciate your help."

"I'll put everything in the truck and drop them off to your house."

"Just put them in the garage," Abraham instructed. "I need to meet with someone later tonight—do you think you'll be around to drive me?"

"Sure," Shadow responded. "I'm here for whatever you need me to do."

"You're a good man."

"I JUST SAW Shadow leaving your office. How did he take the news?" Sophia inquired as she approached his desk.

"Actually, he'll be moving to North Carolina along with us."

She gasped in surprise. "Really? How did this come about?"

"He offered to come. I told him I couldn't afford to keep him on, but he said he isn't worried about money." Abraham rose to his feet. "I don't know about you, but I actually think it's a great idea. The truth is that I feel much safer whenever he's around." He studied Sophia's expression. "What do you think?"

"I'm fine with it." Sophia folded her arms across her chest. "I just wish we could leave like right now. I'm so over Dallas. I've never been so humiliated."

"What's wrong?"

"We've been getting calls all day. They either threaten or call us frauds. One caller said he ordered the healing cloths, and nothing happened. He wants all the money he sent us back with interest."

"Good luck with that," Abraham said with a sigh. "I have an appointment with the bankruptcy attorney Robert referred. I don't see any other way out of this."

"So now we're broke," Sophia exclaimed. "This is the worst time of my life."

Abraham was astonished how his wife always found a way to make his troubles all about her.

———

HE HUNG UP THE PHONE.

Abraham McCormick was leaving town, but he wasn't surprised. The man was nothing more than a coward.

"You won't be able to get away from me," he whispered to the empty room. "Wherever you go, there I will be also. I will follow you the end of the earth. You will never be free of me."

He chuckled. "Til' death do us part."

He picked up a dart and tossed it. It landed in the middle of Abraham's face. He ripped the photo off the wall, tossing it into the trash.

Chapter Six

Three months later

Cynthia drove past the Tahlequah sign in the foothills of the Ozark Mountains. She thought back to the last time she'd come home. It had been a while. Tahlequah was the capital to two Cherokee tribes, the Keetoowah Band and the Cherokee Nation.

There was a time when she wanted nothing more than to be as far away from Cherokee County, but since the accident —she no longer felt safe anywhere but home with her parents. After the surgeon put her bones back together, she had to endure several facial reconstruction surgeries to address the visible incisions, cuts and scars on her skin.

Although Cynthia considered the end results successful, the emotional ramifications such as anxiety, depression and anger were her constant companions.

Cynthia drove through the downtown area, then felt compelled to stop at Northeastern State University, the oldest institution of higher learning in Oklahoma where she'd spent her freshman year. Most of the students were off campus due to the Thanksgiving holiday.

After the rape, she transferred to the University of Oklahoma to study journalism. Cynthia accomplished her goal of becoming an anchorwoman, but her career had been cut short by an unknown assailant who sought to put an end to her life.

Cynthia pulled out of the parking lot and headed to her parent's completely renovated house. Her mother had sent her pictures but this would be her first time seeing it in person.

She drove up the driveway of a custom home overlooking the Illinois River Valley and located on four acres of park-like grounds. Her parents bought the property after Cynthia graduated from college. Her father had the original house gutted and renovated as an anniversary gift to her mother.

She fell in love as soon as she walked through the front door. Cynthia admired the floor to ceiling fireplace situated in a vaulted great room, which also featured large windows welcoming in lots of natural sunlight.

"Mama," she called out.

"I'm in the kitchen, sweetie."

"I'm putting my stuff in the bedroom and I'll be right there."

Cynthia took the stairs to the second level. She walked past the master suite to a bedroom at the other end of the hallway. She rolled her luggage into the room, then went back downstairs.

Cynthia entered the well-appointed gourmet kitchen with gorgeous granite counter tops and beautiful oak wood cabinets and flooring. "Hey Mama."

The two women embraced.

"I'm so glad you're here. I hope you like your room. I've incorporated your favorite colors."

Her heart warmed at her mother's thoughtfulness. "Mama, it's beautiful but you didn't have to go through all that trouble."

"I enjoyed every minute of it," Tracy stated.

"I'm so glad to get away from Dallas," Cynthia said. She hoped the nightmares would vanish now that she was no longer in Texas where there were no constant reminders of Abraham McCormick.

Tracy surveyed her daughter's face. "You look great. Your doctors did a wonderful job."

"Thank you, Mama."

Cynthia glanced around. "Do you need help with dinner?"

Tracy shook her head. "I'm almost done. You sit right there and just keep me company."

Cynthia sat in one of the counter-height chairs. "I've already sent out my resume to a couple of places. I hope to find something quickly. My savings is pretty much gone. My medical insurance covered most of it, but there was still quite a bit of out-of-pocket expenses."

"Your dad and I can help you."

"Noo… I'll be fine, Mama. I'm just saying I need to find a job."

The telephone rang.

Tracy answered on the third ring. "Hello…"

After a brief pause she said, "Sam's not here right now. Let me grab a pen and I'll write down your number."

When she hung up, Cynthia said, "You do know you have Caller ID?"

Tracy waved her hand in dismissal. "I don't think about that stuff. I take messages the old-fashioned way. Even if they leave a voice message—I still write it down."

"Dad told me that the renovations in your bathroom are finished," Cynthia said. "I can't wait to see it."

Her mother smiled. "I love my spa bath. We found this cute curved tub—I had to have it."

"What did Dad say?"

"He refuses to bathe in it. Says he'll just stick to the shower. He thinks it looks too feminine."

Cynthia chuckled. "I'm not surprised."

"I tried to get him to join me in the tub last night…"

"Okay… TMI…"

"My point is that it will hold both of us comfortably. It's very nice."

Cynthia got up and strolled over to the enclosed patio. "This is very nice and private."

"Exactly what we were striving for—privacy."

While her mother finished cooking, Cynthia went back to her room to get settled.

She opened her suitcase and began to put away her clothes.

Sophia glanced over at the mirror hanging over the dresser. She walked over, took it down, then resumed hanging up her clothing.

———

CYNTHIA WAS ABOUT to join her parents for dinner when she received a phone call.

"Nadine did what?" Shaking her head, she said, "No, I don't believe that. Something must have happened to make her do that…"

"What happened?" her father inquired when she sat down at the table.

"Nadine dropped the charges against Abraham. I don't understand why she'd do that. She was positive that he was the person who attacked her last year." Cynthia placed the napkin in her lap.

"She was walking to her car after work when he basically punched her in the face and raped her. At the time, she had no idea who her attacker was—until she saw some advertisement for an event his church was having. When she saw the picture of Abraham... she called me, and she was hysterical. I spent the night at her place because Nadine was traumatized all over again."

"So why did she drop the charges?"

"Dad, I don't know," Cynthia said. "I called her a few minutes ago, but she refused to talk to me about it. I think she's scared."

Her mother wiped her mouth with the edge of her napkin. "I agree with Cynthia. I'm sure she believes that Abraham McCormick had something to do with your accident plus the other women dropping the charges like that... she's afraid."

"If guilty, he will get what he deserves," her father stated. "McCormick won't be able to outrun the consequences of his actions."

"Why don't we change the subject?" Tracy suggested. "There's a writing contest for middle schoolers being sponsored by the Cherokee Nation. Maybe you could be one of our judges."

"What's the topic this year?" Cynthia asked.

They're writing either a poem or short story on *How Does the Story of the Phoenix Bird Apply Today?*"

"Wow," she murmured. "That's going to be interesting. Since I began that story on Abraham McCormick, everything in my life has burned to ashes it seems. I've had to face the fire in all the surgeries… this story seems to really echo my life right now."

"Out of the ashes a new Phoenix is born."

"So, a group of kids in middle school are going to write about a bird that lives 500 years, then makes a nest and sets itself on fire and is reborn—they have to apply this story to what's happening today."

Her mother nodded. "Yes."

"I actually like this idea of a new, stronger Phoenix emerging from the ashes—it inspires hope; signifies renewal and resurrection."

"Some believe that the phoenix dying, then rising gloriously from the ashes to fly away symbolizes Christ's death, resurrection and his ascension into Heaven."

Cynthia chuckled. "I don't know about that. Sounds nice, I guess. I'm sure these men of the cloth like McCormick would find a way to spin that story into a money-making scheme."

"I know we didn't raise you in church, but I wish I'd taken you more," Tracy stated. "You have such a negative perception of pastors. There are some good ones out there."

"Mama, do you watch the news? Or read the paper? It's more a gimmick than a ministry. That's what I see. Maybe there was a time when pastors were truly men of God, but today—they all have some ploy to fleece their congregations. And then there are the ones who promise material wealth to those who plant *financial seeds*. I admit I don't read the Bible very often, but from what I've read—God rewards those who live according to His Word, not just give tithes and offerings."

"Not all ministers are like that, Cynthia."

"I haven't met one that wasn't," she retorted. "Look at Abraham McCormick. He's giving people *healing* cloths and begging for money at the same time. Then when he isn't doing that, he's attacking women when they're defenseless and trying to take out people who expose his dirty deeds."

"You know forgiveness strikes a mighty blow, *Uwetsi ageyv*," her father said, using the Cherokee word for daughter. "When you can forgive the person, who has wronged you and look upon them with compassion—you weld more power than you can ever imagine."

"I understand what you're saying," Cynthia responded. "I'm just not there yet. Maybe one day I'll be able to forgive, but that day has not come."

Her father wiped his mouth with his napkin. "Tomorrow isn't promised to any of us."

Cynthia took a sip of her water. "It's not easy. Every time I look into a mirror and I see this person... speaking of mirrors, Dad can you please take the one out of my room? I've already taken it off the wall."

"Sure," Samuel responded. "I'll remove it tonight."

"You are still my very beautiful daughter."

"Thank you, Mama. It's just weird for me right now. I feel like me—but whenever I look in the person I see that the person I used to be is gone forever."

"Maybe the physical part, but you're still very much *you*," Samuel stated.

"That's just it. I'm no longer me. I'm no longer Cynthia Highcloud."

"Then who are you?"

"I'm that Phoenix bird, Mama. I've been reborn but I just don't have my wings yet." She finished her dinner, then said, "I'm going to pass on dessert. When you and Dad are done, I'll clean the kitchen."

Cynthia pushed away from the table. "I'm going to try and get Nadine to talk to me."

In her bedroom, she placed another call to her friend.

"Cynthia, I've made my decision so just stop trying to change my mind."

"I'm only trying to make sense of this."

"I'm tired and I can't deal with the stress. I'm moving on with my life."

"I'm sorry, Nadine. I hate that you have to deal with this craziness, but I'm glad that you spoke up. It was a very brave thing to do."

"I'm done, Cynthia. I mean it."

"I know that you're scared. I can hear it in your voice. Did someone threaten you?"

"No," Nadine uttered. "Seriously, I just want out. Pastor McCormick is going to walk away unscathed. Can't you see that? He's another Gerald Lassiter."

Unless you speak up, Cynthia wanted to voice, but she didn't want to upset her friend. "I can't change your mind, Nadine. Although I'm disappointed, I'll support your decision."

"I know you don't agree with it, but I have to do this for me."

"Okay."

"Sabre said the same thing, but I know she doesn't approve of my decision either. I appreciate that you two aren't trying to bully me into changing my mind."

"We would never do that," Cynthia stated. "I just want you to be okay."

"I will be. This is what's best for me right now. I need to move on."

The pain in Nadine's voice called out to Cynthia, filling her with anger. She hated what this was doing to her friend and it frustrated her that she couldn't do anything to help. She hated that Abraham would get away with his crimes just like Gerald.

———

RALEIGH, *North Carolina*

"I never thought I'd ever say this, but I'm actually to be back in the triangle," Sophia said. "It feels good."

"I'm glad," Abraham responded. "I didn't want you around all of that drama back in Texas."

"This is a chance for a new beginning." Sophia glanced around the room. "My mom will be here shortly. We're going shopping. I want to get a few things for this place, especially if we're going to live here for the next year or so."

He agreed.

Abraham knew it wasn't easy for Sophia to have to live in the former home of her deceased aunt. Her mother's intention to rent the home came at the perfect time. This would allow them to save money and rebuild their lives.

"This is the perfect place for us, I guess," he said. "It even comes with a basement apartment for Shadow. I may not be able to pay him, but at least he has a place to stay."

"My aunt used the rental revenue for the upkeep of the house. When my uncle died, she used some of the insurance money to pay off the mortgage." Sophia picked her purse and the car keys. "What we do from this moment forward... it has to be done with care. We can't let the nightmare in Dallas happen all over again."

"You're right, sweetheart."

"This time though, we're going to need a security team," Sophia stated as she headed toward the door. "We have to keep people in check."

"I'll put Shadow in charge. One thing I know is that he's loyal to me."

"Good." She planted a kiss on his lips. "Behave while I'm gone. The same rules apply here. No tramps in my house *evah*."

Abraham laughed. "Now you know I'm not crazy."

"If you were smart, I'd be the only woman in your life. You wouldn't be running around here like a dog in heat. I knew what you were when I married you and I promised you then—I'd never try to change you and I meant that."

"That's why I adore you, sweetheart."

"I'll see you in a couple of hours." She paused in her tracks. The hair on the back of her neck stood up and she became increasingly uneasy.

"Sophia..."

She turned to look at Abraham.

"What's wrong?" he asked.

Sophia swallowed hard, trying to manage a feeble answer. "I just felt the strangest sensation. I felt like someone was watching me."

Abraham stepped out onto the porch, his eyes searching. "I don't see anything out of the norm."

"I guess I'm still a bit jumpy."

There was a pensive shimmer in the shadow of her eyes. He escorted her to the car. "Do you want me to drive you?"

Sophia shook her head no. "I'll be fine. Maybe you and Shadow can finish putting up the light fixtures in the kitchen. The original ones hanging in there now are just hideous."

He kissed her. "I'll take care of it."

"No weapons formed against me shall prosper," Abraham whispered.

⊏▬▬⊐

HE BROKE into a grin when Sophia drove past him, oblivious to his presence. It pleased him that they were getting settled into their home. It meant life was becoming normal once again—they were comfortable.

This is exactly what he wanted. He wanted them to think that things were going to get better for them. And when it did —he would strike.

His attention shifted when he caught sight of a tall muscular man coming from the side of the house.

Abraham bought his guard dog along.

Perfect.

Chapter Seven

Cynthia waited until after the first of the year to aggressively find a job.

The lack of call backs after her first round of interviews, left Cynthia feeling somewhat down. It was also a blow to her already fragile self-esteem.

"Why don't you apply at the University?" her mother suggested. "Or teach at the high school level?"

"At this point, I'd take anything," Cynthia said. "I'm ready to go back to work."

"Have you talked to Nadine lately? She's been on my mind."

"She's getting back to her old self, I guess. She doesn't talk about anything that happened—she doesn't want to discuss it. Sabre and I agree that this isn't necessarily a good thing, but there's nothing we can do about it."

"You're doing all you can at this point," Tracy stated. "She'll come to you and Sabre when she's ready. If she doesn't then you have to respect her decision."

"I guess I'll go send out another hundred copies of my resume."

"Be encouraged."

"Thanks Mama."

Cynthia went upstairs and turned on the television in her room.

She watched the news before switching the channel. She loved being a reporter and she missed it, but she wasn't ready to go back to championing the wrongs in the world. She was still too angry and hungry for revenge.

She couldn't just let go and trust God to take care of Abraham. She'd done that with Gerald, and nothing happened. He was able to go on to play in the NFL and have a family while her once glowing youthful happiness faded.

AFTER BEING BACK in Raleigh for a couple of months, Sophia began to feel a calm in her spirit. She was grateful they were able to include the lawsuits from several members of their former church in the bankruptcy.

It still amazed Sophia how Abraham was able to go about life unbothered, despite all he'd been accused of—he told her it was because he was innocent. He refused to walk around with his head hung in shame. Sophia admired his fortitude.

When Abraham descended the stairs dressed in a charcoal-colored suit with a mint-green shirt, she asked, "Where are you going?"

"I have an appointment but after that I might ride around town for a bit… get reacquainted. A lot has changed since we left," Abraham said.

"Give me a minute and I'll go with you."

"Sweetheart, you don't have to do that," he responded a little too quickly for her liking.

"Do you really think I'm that stupid? We haven't been back here a hot minute and you've already found some tramp to be a repository for your lust." With a shake of her head, Sophia uttered, "I'm so done with you right now."

"I'm just—"

She cut him off by saying, "Don't insult me by lying, Abraham. Remember, I'm the woman who broke up your first marriage. The only difference is that I'm not going *anywhere*. I don't care how many hoes you run through. We're married for life."

"Where did that come from?"

"Some woman called to check on you the night you were shot. I'm assuming she was the one you had been with when it happened. They don't need to call my house. You better teach them to stay in their lane." She turned away from him.

He came up behind her, his hands on her shoulders. "I'm not going to see another woman, sweetheart. I'm meeting with the pastor of Holy Cross Christian Center."

She turned, facing him. "Why didn't you mention this before?"

"I didn't want to get your hopes up. Joel Connor is stepping down and he thought I might be interested in taking his place."

"That's great news." She smiled but it quickly disappeared. "Does he know about everything that happened in Texas?"

Abraham nodded. "He believes in me, Sophia. Connor told me that he sees something in me that I've yet to see in myself."

Nodding in agreement, she said, "He's right. I've been telling you the same thing for years."

"When I look in the mirror… all I see are my flaws."

"Then you need to learn to look deeper—past your imperfections."

Abraham stole a peek at his watch. "I have to go. I don't want to be late for my meeting."

"I'm sure it'll go well," Sophia stated. "I can't wait to hear about it when you come home. We need something good to happen right now."

"I've been in prayer ever since I got the email." Abraham smiled. "I have a good feeling about this."

"You're the most positive person I've ever met," Sophia said. "You always manage to see a bright side in everything."

"I must've gotten that from my parents. They never let a dark moment linger." He checked his watch. "I have to go, my love. We'll talk when I get back. Shadow's in his apartment if you need him."

"Go, don't keep the man waiting," Sophia urged.

She desperately hoped Abraham would return with good news. They needed something like this to happen—something good. Something to get them back in a position of leadership. Abraham was meant to be a leader. Nothing else would do, nor would Sophia allow him to settle for anything less.

Upstairs, Sophia treated herself to a soothing bubble bath scented with lavender oil.

Afterward, she slipped on sexy black lingerie when the sound of laughter captured her attention.

Sophia glanced out of her bedroom window in time to glimpse Shadow escorting a woman into the apartment below. He peered upward, catching sight of her.

Their gaze met and held until she broke the stare by closing the blinds. Sophia felt a streak of jealousy but didn't quite understand why.

He *is* attractive, she mused, in a sullen kind of way.

Sophia glanced over at the clock on the nightstand. Abraham had been gone for an hour. She wanted to call him to find out what was going on but didn't want to disturb her husband if he were still in a meeting.

We need this to work, dear Lord. Abraham needs to pastor this church.

Two hours passed, and Sophia's irritation spread like a wildfire growing out of control. She was pretty sure the meeting had long ended.

"Abraham, you liar…" she uttered.

Sophia tossed his pillow across the room before turning off the lamp. Her eyes traveled to the clock once again. "I bet there was never a meeting in the first place."

She wasn't sure what angered her more—the fact that Abraham had gotten her hopes up about the leadership position or that he was out messing around with some tramp.

CYNTHIA WAITED for Adrienne to answer her call. She toyed with the idea that if she could get her to stick to her story, then maybe Nadine wouldn't feel alone in her quest for justice.

"Adrienne… hello. This is Cynthia. I wanted to call and check on you."

"I'm fine. How are *you?*"

"I'm taking it one day at a time," she responded. "I want you to know that I believe you. If you…"

"I'm trying to move on with my life, Cynthia," Adrienne interjected. "I never should've said anything. I don't know how he did it, but Pastor McCormick made me look like a liar. I would never lie about something like this. I left that bar with him. We went to a hotel and he drugged me... I..." her voice broke.

"I believe you. That's why I don't think you should give up your claim."

"It happened a long time ago, Cynthia. It's my word against his. He's been able to discredit all of us."

"You can't back down, Adrienne. *You shouldn't back down.* You can't let McCormick win."

"Cynthia, I don't want what happened to you to happen to me. He's a very dangerous man. The night he raped me," Adrienne paused a heartbeat before continuing. "He had this look in his eyes. I really thought he was going to kill me."

"If he remains fee to walk the streets, Adrienne, he could hurt someone else."

"I tried, Cynthia. Now I'm out here looking like a scorned woman or worse—a liar."

"Why are you so sure that it was St. Patrick's Day?" she asked.

"Because I wrote about it in my journal. I wrote how that day is one I won't ever forget because of what happened. It's the one day I dread every year."

Chapter Eight

"Good morning," Abraham greeted when he strolled into the kitchen.

Sophia pretended she didn't hear him. Dressed in a lavender terrycloth robe, she moved around the kitchen as if he didn't exist.

"Sweetheart…" he knew there was a strong chance that she'd be upset, but the way Sophia stomped around, rolling her eyes and clanging pots. She was furious with him.

"Don't even," she interjected, her tone harsh. "Don't talk to me. I can't stand look at you right now."

"I was with Pastor Connor, Sophia. We got to talking and well… it ran late. I'm sorry I didn't call you to let you know I'd be out late. I should have."

She kept her back to him.

"I'm going to be the new pastor of Holy Cross," Abraham announced, hoping she would calm down. "Connor plans to announce it in a couple of weeks."

Sophia faced him. "So, you weren't lying?"

He shook his head. "Connor invited us over for dinner tomorrow night. He wants his wife to meet us."

"*Why*? Do we need her approval?"

Abraham chuckled. "No. It's just a friendly little dinner."

"Just needed to know if I need to wear my game face, babe. That's all."

"We always wear our game faces, Sophia." He placed his arms around her. "Now can you stop being angry with me?"

Nodding, Sophia smiled. "I tried to wait up for you."

"I'll make it up to you. Tonight, we're going to that favorite Italian place of yours."

She hugged him. "I'm so proud of you."

Abraham kissed her. "Thank you for always believing in me."

A few minutes later, they sat down for breakfast. Sophia had prepared spinach and mushroom omelets, bacon and fresh fruit for them.

"This news couldn't have come at a better time." She sliced into her omelet. "I thought I'd have to actually find a job." Sophia looked over at him. "You did discuss salary, right?"

Abraham nodded. "It's starting at $80,000 a year for now."

"That's not nearly enough to support our lifestyle."

"Sophia, we're bankrupt. It's a whole lot better than nothing. Once we take over, I believe we can double the membership—then we can ask for an increase in salary."

"I suppose you're right," she responded.

"Sweetheart, it's only a temporary setback. Just remember that. It won't always be like this. And the other thing is that we don't have to pay rent. We can rebuild our savings."

Sophia smiled. "You will always find a silver lining."

When they finished eating, Abraham offered to clean the kitchen while she went up to get dressed.

Upstairs, Sophia padded barefoot into the bathroom.

After her shower, she toweled off and strolled into the walk-in closet in search of something to wear.

Sophia decided on a pair of black yoga pants and a light yellow top with black and yellow sneakers.

On the way out, she caught sight of the tousled shirt Abraham had worn the night before.

Listening to her gut, she grabbed it and put it up to her nose, catching a whiff of her husband's cologne mixed with a light floral scent.

Her instincts were right. Abraham may have been telling the truth about his meeting, but he hadn't come straight home.

"Focus on the plan," she whispered, her hands clenching and unclenching. "You know the man you married. Just stay focused."

Sophia grabbed her keys and rushed down the stairs. Her kickboxing class started in less than an hour. She wanted to arrive early to warm-up.

She ran into Shadow outside.

"Morning, Mrs. McCormick."

"Good morning," she responded. Sophia paused mid-stride to add, "It's okay to call me by my first name. We needn't be so formal, Shadow. You're practically family now."

He gave a small smile. "Alright... Sophia."

She grinned. "That's much better."

"Your husband wants me to drive you wherever you need to go."

Sophia handed him her keys.

Outside, he held the car door open for her.

She eased into the car, very aware that Shadow's gaze was

on her. She wasn't offended by his attention, especially today. If Abraham insisted on cheating—two could play this game.

"I'm so glad you're driving me. I don't like I-40 in the mornings. My anxiety kicks in when traffic is heavy."

He remained silent during the drive to the gym while Sophia read through her email.

When they arrived, she got out, saying, "Thank you so much."

"It's my pleasure, Mrs... uh... Sophia."

Sophia touched his arm. "I have to tell you that I'm so glad you decided to come to North Carolina with us. I feel so much safer with you being here."

"Nothing will happen to you while I'm around."

She believed he meant every word.

Sophia pretended to be focused on her phone, but her mind was elsewhere. Since Abraham clearly didn't have a faithful bone in his body—why should she? She loved him and divorce wasn't an option.

There's nothing to stop me from having a little fun, she decided.

Sophia stole a peek at Shadow.

He was a very handsome man and the cologne he wore, wafted to her nostrils, riding the breeze blowing from the air conditioner. She knew that he was attracted to her—she could see it in his gaze.

She broke into a tiny smile. *This was going to be easy.*

Before he drove away, he asked, "What time should I pick you up?"

"After kickboxing, I'm going down to the pool for a few laps... come back in a couple of hours," Sophia responded. "You're welcome to join me."

His eyes widened in surprise. "Maybe some other time."

She chuckled as she made her way through the doors of

the gym facility. There was nothing wrong with harmless flirting. Her sex life with Abraham was great, but she was starting to feel lonely.

Sophia hated feeling this way because it made her appear weak, in her opinion, which is why she would voice her feelings to Abraham. She had mastered the act of suffering in silence.

⊏▭▭⊐

"DYLAN'S FLIGHT should land in about fifteen minutes," Cynthia announced as she helped her mother with the seating arrangements for an upcoming fundraising event. It had been three months since his last visit. She was looking forward to seeing him. Although she didn't know what to expect. Their communication over the past few months had become strained and less frequent.

It was mostly on Cynthia's part. Things just weren't the same between the two of them.

"You don't sound very happy about it," Tracy said as she checked off the names on her guest list.

"Mama, I'm thrilled he's coming home. I've missed him." It was true, but she was also insecure. Dylan said all the right things whenever they Skyped, texted and emailed each other, but Cynthia felt like something was missing.

"Did you ever send Dylan a picture?"

"I did," Cynthia responded. "But I'm sure it won't compare to seeing me in person."

"Dylan fell in love with the woman you are on the inside, Cynthia."

"I guess we'll soon find out if that's true."

Cynthia walked outside to the porch when Dylan's rental

car pulled into the driveway. He got out and strolled toward her.

"You look so different," was the first words out of his mouth. Not *I love you* or *I missed you.*

"I know," Cynthia responded. "That's why it's hard to look at myself in a mirror."

They walked inside the house holding hands.

Once they were seated, Cynthia suddenly didn't know what to say.

"You're quiet."

"This is awkward for me," she admitted. "I don't want to keep saying the same thing over and over again, but the gist of it is that I'm angry, Dylan. I loved the way I used to look—flaws and all. Initially, I thought maybe I'd start to feel more like me after the bruising and swelling went down, but I don't. I know this has to be a bit weird for you as well. I guess maybe we should talk about it."

"Babe I did some research so that I could understand what you're going through."

Cynthia inclined her head. "What did you find out?"

"That people who have gone through something like this —healing is a long-term process and adaptation. I need you to know that I think you're still beautiful, Cynthia. You're still you."

"That's just it, Dylan. I don't feel like me anymore." She sat in the chair, her slender fingers tensed in her lap.

"Have you considered talking to someone like a psychiatrist?" he inquired. "Your doctor mentioned it a while back."

Cynthia shook her head. "I don't need to talk to a psychiatrist. I'm good."

"But you're not."

She flinched at the tone of his voice. "It's going to take

some time, Dylan. Maybe if you were here with me instead of in Cairo—you'd have a better understanding of what I'm dealing with."

"If I could be here, I would," Dylan said. "But I'm not sure my being here would make any difference. You live with your parents. Your mom told me that you don't really go out much."

"My mother talks too much."

"We're all just trying to help," Dylan interjected. "From what I understand, it's important to give yourself time to adjust to changes in your appearance, but at some point, you need to get out of this house. Like tonight... why don't we go out? You can show me around town."

"I don't know," Cynthia responded. "I'm not sure I'm ready for that."

"Babe, I'll be with you. It'll do you some good to just have dinner somewhere. What about that steakhouse you told me about? You say you go there every time you come home."

"Cherokee Station?"

Dylan nodded. "I keep thinking about that chocolate pie you used to always rave about."

"I haven't been there in a while," she stated.

"So, what about dinner there tonight?"

He was right. She couldn't keep hiding at home. Besides, she was in Cherokee, Oklahoma, 350 miles away from Dallas. She was safe.

Cynthia nodded. "Let's do it, but first... Dylan, there's something I need to discuss with you."

"What is it?"

"I think we should call our engagement off for now."

His surprise was evident. "Why?"

"I can't think about planning a wedding or getting married in the emotional state I'm in. I hope you understand."

"Are you sure about this?" Dylan inquired.

Cynthia chose her words carefully. "I'm trying very hard to adjust to this new me and it's going to take a while. The old me died that night."

"I loved that woman."

"I know you did." Cynthia took his hand into her own. "But Dylan, you have to know she's never coming back. This is who I am now."

"I want to get to know this new you."

"And you will," Cynthia stated. "We have time without the pressure of planning a wedding. Besides, we both need this adjustment period."

Dylan nodded in agreement. "I know you're right. I just feel like I'm losing you."

"You're not," Cynthia assured him.

He kissed her.

"Do you feel like you just kissed a stranger?"

He chuckled. "No, they were definitely your lips."

Cynthia wasn't sure she quite believed him. There was something in his gaze. Something she couldn't identify.

"I have a Skype meeting with my boss," Dylan said, "so I need to get going. I'll be here around 6:30 to pick you up."

She smiled. "I'll be ready. You're going to love Cherokee Station."

He hugged her. "We'll figure all this out, babe."

She awarded him a tiny smile. "I know."

Cynthia stood in the window watching as he drove away.

"How did it go?" Tracy asked.

She turned to face her mother. "We decided to take a break. The engagement is off for now. It was my decision,

Mama. Like I told Dylan, I am not the same woman I was before the accident. That's the person he fell in love with—we need to get to know each other all over again."

"You may wear a different face, but your spirit is still the same."

Shaking her head, Cynthia disagreed. "Dylan and I are going out for dinner. We're going to Cherokee Station."

Her mother grinned. "That's wonderful. I'm glad you're getting out of this house."

"Well, the first thing I need to do is figure out something with my hair." Cynthia walked toward the stairs. "Wish me luck."

"You should wear it pulled into a low bun to show off the neckline of that dress you just bought. I still can't believe you found it on Amazon, but it'll be perfect for your date. Use the mirror in my room."

"Thanks, Mama. That works for me. Now I just have to figure out jewelry and shoes."

When she was dressed, Cynthia ventured into her parents' room. She eyed her reflection in the mirror.

"You look stunning," her mother said.

"I don't see any scarring," she murmured. "I don't know what I expected. It's still going to take some getting used to—this face."

Cynthia looked at her mother and smiled.

"I want you to have fun tonight," Tracy said. "Maybe this is what you and Dylan need to help you reconnect."

"Dinner at Cherokee Station is not going to make me change my mind about the engagement, Mama."

JOEL AND MARY CONNOR greeted them in the foyer.

"It's so nice to meet you, Sophia," Mary said with a welcoming smile.

"Nice to meet you as well."

They were seated in the living room when the doorbell sounded.

"Our other guests have arrived," Joel said. "I want you to meet Eli and Otis. They're my associate pastors."

A slender woman dressed in a black sheath dress with a short pixie cut hairstyle entered in front of a man who looked to be about 6 feet 6 or 7 inches tall.

"That's Eli Carpenter," Abraham whispered to Sophia. "He used to play for the Clippers."

She surveyed Lenni Carpenter. The woman was not exactly what Sophia considered pretty—she was striking. Her dress and shoes weren't cheap but understated. She had a quiet elegance about her except for the three or four carat engagement ring worn on her left hand.

The doorbell sounded a few minutes later.

Joel opened the door and ushered in another couple.

Sophia guessed this had to be Otis and his wife.

Mary made the introductions. "This is Otis and Olympia Robinson. And this couple her Eli and Lenni Carpenter."

Abraham and Sophia stood up to greet each of them.

"I wanted you all to meet," Joel said, "because Abraham McCormick will be taking my place as Senior Pastor of Holy Cross."

"Congratulations," Otis and his wife said in unison.

Eli glanced at his wife before saying, "We are very fortunate to have you as part of the Holy Cross family."

Sophia noticed that while Lenni hadn't uttered a word, her expression spoke volumes.

Mary went to make sure everything was ready.

The men gathered in one corner of the living room to talk, leaving Sophia alone with Olympia and Lenni.

"So where are you from?" Olympia inquired.

"I'm originally from here," Sophia said, "but we moved here from Dallas."

"We're so glad to have you at Holy Cross, aren't we Lenni?"

Clutching her pearls, she responded, "Why, of course."

Sophia pasted on a smile. "Thank you, both."

Ten minutes later, they were all gathered around a heavy oak dining table discussing Abraham's transition to Holy Cross.

Lenni didn't have a whole lot to contribute to the women's conversation during dinner.

Sour grapes, Sophia decided. She must have hoped Eli would've become the leader, but for whatever reason—he wasn't selected. It wasn't Abraham's problem nor was it hers. Lenni would just have to deal with it.

When it was time for dessert to be served, Lenni cited a bad headache and decided it was best for them to leave.

"I'm so sorry, but I'm just not feeling well. This headache's getting worse."

Eli looked a bit irritated but had no choice but to take Lenni home.

Otis and Olympia stayed for another hour but had to leave to pick up their children.

Abraham and Sophia made ready to walk out with them, but Joel asked them to stay.

"We're thrilled about Abraham taking over the church," Mary told Sophia while their husbands were behind closed doors in Joel's office. "When my husband prayed over who should succeed him, Abraham was the only person to come to mind." She paused, then asked, "I'm pretty good at reading people. Is there something you'd like to ask me?"

Sophia met her gaze. "Yes, there is. I'm really surprised by the way your husband embraced Abraham. Most of the pastors we once considered close friends will have nothing to do with him."

Mary smiled. "You're much younger so you won't remember this, but my husband went through something similar. He was accused of having sex with a woman in our church. She even claimed she was carrying his child. We lost more than half our members... it was a terrible time for us. Not only were we ostracized by the church community—the public attacked us, too."

"Was it true?" Sophia asked.

Shrugging, Mary responded, "That same girl miscarried or, so it was claimed. I really don't know if she was telling the truth about anything. My husband said he never touched her, and I chose to believe him. He was forced out of that church. We had to start over but look where we are now. There's no shame in starting over, Sophia. Sometimes it's a necessity."

"It doesn't feel good."

"No, it doesn't."

"Abraham has handled this whole situation with such class," Sophia stated. "He knows that he's innocent and doesn't act contrary to that."

"That's one of the qualities my husband likes where Abraham is concerned."

"What about Eli and Otis?" Sophia questioned. "Why weren't either of them chosen? I know that Lenni is clearly disappointed that her husband wasn't chosen."

"Mary smiled. "I noticed that as well. She no more had a

headache that my having one. But to answer your question—God spoke your husband's name into his heart. For this season, Abraham is to lead Holy Cross."

"So, what do you think about the Connors?" Abraham inquired when they were on the way home.

"I really like them. They understand what we're dealing with and I appreciate the fact that they are so supportive."

Abraham nodded in agreement.

"Otis and his wife seemed really nice—she's a bit chatty, but I like her," Sophia said. "But Eli and Lenni… I haven't made up my mind about them yet."

"They seem okay to me," he responded. "Olympia seems a bit off to me."

Sophia laughed. "She is a little special."

"This is it," Abraham said. "We're on our way back up."

"Nobody is going to stop us this time," she vowed.

Chapter Nine

"So, does anyone know where McCormick went?" Cynthia asked, switching her phone from one ear to the other. "How does a man who was accused of drugging and raping women just disappear? I know he was cleared of the charges, but surely, someone has to know where he is…"

"Why don't you just let this go?" Sabre suggested. "He's disappeared—maybe he left the country. Regardless, I'm pretty sure we'll never hear from him again."

"I don't think we're that lucky," Cynthia countered. "The fact that Abraham's been able to get away with so much, will make him arrogant. He'll get comfortable."

"I love you like a sister so I'm going to tell you that you need to drop this. Forget about Abraham McCormick. Leave him to the Lord."

"I'm not sure I can do that, Sabre. I'm tired of men like him doing vile things and just walking away without consequences. I want this man to pay for what he's done."

"You're beginning to sound like a broken record."

"Wow...," Cynthia uttered. "Sabre, I'll talk to you later."

"Hey, don't be mad..."

"Seriously, I need to go. I have a phone interview coming up within the hour and I need to mentally prepare for it."

Why didn't anybody understand her feelings?

———

THIS WAS Abraham's first solo trip out of town for church business. Although she knew he was traveling with Pastor Connor, Sophia suspected that he was not without female companionship.

He loved women. In truth, Sophia considered that Abraham possibly had a bit of a sexual addiction. Her hand placed over her smooth, taut belly, she thought perhaps if she was a real woman—she alone would be enough for him.

Needing some reassurance of her womanhood, she decided to pay a visit to Shadow.

Sophia went downstairs and knocked.

The door opened almost immediately.

"I hope you don't mind me coming here unannounced."

"Not at all," Shadow responded. "What can I do for you?" He stepped aside to let her enter the apartment.

"I was feeling a bit lonely," Sophia confessed, her gaze bouncing around the neat apartment, quickly noting that it was decorated in a minimalistic style. "Have you eaten? I was thinking of grabbing dinner, but I didn't want to eat alone."

"I have some chicken in the oven. You're welcome to join me. It's more than enough."

She smiled. "It does smell delicious. I had no idea you could cook."

"A man's gotta eat," he responded.

"Did someone teach you?"

Shadow nodded. "My mom. She had me learning how to cook when I was around twelve years old. She worked nights and I had to look out for my little brother."

"I make a pretty good salad," Sophia announced. "Do you have the ingredients?"

"See what you can find in the refrigerator."

In a matter of minutes, Sophia had mixed a baby spinach salad together with cranberries, walnuts, and gorgonzola cheese. "I think I saw bottles of ranch and raspberry dressing in there. I think the raspberry is perfect with this."

Shadow looked impressed.

"Why didn't you go with Abraham?" Sophia asked when they sat down to eat half an hour later. "You're his bodyguard." She took a long sip of red wine.

"I thought it better that I stay here," Shadow responded. "He's with Pastor Connor, so he's not alone. Besides, he told me that you thought you were being watched. He was worried that you'd be afraid if left alone in the house."

She chuckled. "How sweet, but there's another reason why he left you behind. I'm pretty sure he has another traveling companion as well. Shadow, just an FYI… I'm not ignorant of my husband's affairs."

"You deserve to be treated like a queen."

Sophia smiled seductively. "So, if I were yours, I'd never have to worry about you being unfaithful?" When he didn't respond immediately, she continued. "I've seen the way you watch me when you think I'm not paying attention."

His eyes darted to hers. "I respect your marriage, Mrs. McCormick."

She sliced off a sliver of the mouthwatering chicken breast

smothered in a garlic butter sauce and stuck it into her mouth. "This is delicious."

They made small talk while they ate.

"Why did you leave the FBI?" Sophia inquired.

"I wanted to do something different," Shadow responded. "I've always wanted to have my own business specializing in security for high-profile clients. Working for Abraham gives me the experience I need to do that."

"Now that Abraham will be the pastor of Holy Cross, he's going to need a security team."

"He spoke to me about it before he left town."

Sophia wiped her mouth with the edge of her napkin. "That's good. I'm glad he and I are on the same page."

They cleaned the kitchen after they finished eating.

"Thank you for allowing me to show up unannounced and have dinner with you, Shadow. I really appreciate it."

He flashed his beautifully blinding teeth. "It was my pleasure."

She saw that his wide eyes were directly on her large chest. Sophia tossed away the thought that she looked like some desperate chick, throwing my big boobs out there like that. She didn't care at the moment. "I really like you, Shadow." Sophia said, pressing her body against his. "But before this goes any further—there is one rule. Don't go falling in love or anything like that. Abraham and I have our issues, but we are a great team and we've put plans in place that will make us very rich. I've worked too hard to just walk away from my marriage. I hope you understand."

"You have no intentions of leaving your husband. I get it."

"So, do you have a problem with just being my lover?"

Shadow shook his head no. "I can handle it."

"Good," she murmured. "Why don't you show me the bedroom?"

———

"ABRAHAM HAS A NEW CHURCH. I think we should just lay low and let him rise up. He has some ideas that I believe will make him a big as these millionaire mega pastors walking around."

"Really?"

"Yeah. If we're patient… we can destroy him and walk away with all his money."

"I like that plan."

"In order for this to work, you need to leave town. We can't risk him or his wife running into you. You don't have to worry. I'll be here to keep tabs on him."

"So, what's this plan of his?"

"I don't know all the ends and outs yet. As soon as I find out—you'll be the first to know."

"He's gonna pay for what he did?"

"I know."

"I'll leave town, but I want to be kept abreast of everything that happens." He sent a sharp gaze to the man standing before him. "Don't screw me over with this." He escorted his visitor to the door.

"I won't." Tapping the hotel door, he said, "You really need to get out of here. It's too risky with your being in town."

Irritated, he uttered, "I heard you the first time. I'll check out first thing tomorrow morning."

He watched his friend disappear down the long hallway before closing the door. He intended to keep his word. He would leave, but first there was one more thing he needed to take care of.

An hour later, a young woman arrived.

"You came highly recommended," he said. "I hope you won't disappoint me."

She smiled. "I won't. I'm just here to get my coins. I'm Fallon by the way."

"You don't need to worry about who I am." He laid out his instructions. "Keep it professional. Don't let your emotions get involved."

"You don't have to worry. I know what I'm doing."

"I'll be in and out of town, but you can reach me on this number. I'm sure I don't have to tell you discretion is crucial, Fallon."

"I got it."

"Don't disappoint me."

She flashed him a sexy grin. "Trust me... I never disappoint."

Chapter Ten

---

2 years later

Cynthia graded the last of the student papers, then turned off her computer with a long sigh. It wasn't that she didn't enjoy teaching creative writing—it just wasn't her passion. She missed being a reporter.

"Why don't you go back to the television station?" her father inquired a few days before she landed the faculty position at the University of Oklahoma.

"I don't think I can handle that," Cynthia had responded. "I don't look the same. I feel different… it just wouldn't be the way it used to be for me. It would only remind me of everything that happened and I'm trying really hard to move past that nightmare."

"There are thousands of television stations all over the world, *Uwetsi ageyv.*"

"I know, dad. I'm just not ready to make myself a target. McCormick is still out there somewhere. I'm much safer remaining off the grid."

"Why? Because you're going after him."

She nodded. "He's going to resurface sooner or later. I'll be here patiently waiting."

"Be careful to not let your anger overtake you."

Cynthia didn't respond. She respected her father, but she did not agree with him in this situation. She had a right to her anger—a right to let it fester into a slow burn. She wanted the flames of fury to engulf her. She made a personal vow to make Abraham McCormick pay for his crimes. But first, she had to track him down.

———

ABRAHAM AND SOPHIA strolled through their newly renovated church, Holy Cross Healing & Deliverance Ministries. "I love the new name," she told him. "I have to confess that I thought this day would never come."

Abraham eyed his wife. "Sophia, have you no faith in me?"

"I have nothing but faith in you," she responded. "It just seems like it's been forever since we left Texas with our tails tucked between our legs. I'd never been so humiliated in my life—I don't want to ever experience something like that again."

"You won't. Sophia, you have nothing to worry about."

"I hope you're right because I've already found the perfect house for us—it will be new construction."

Smiling, Abraham said, "I can't wait to see it."

"We can stop by the neighborhood right after service today. I want you to see the model. The floorplans don't really do it justice."

"I haven't seen you this happy in a long time," Abraham

said. "I thought I was going to lose you after everything happened. Especially when I was forced to file bankruptcy."

"We were publicly shamed. It's taken some time for me to get over it." She turned to look directly at him. "You got careless, Abraham. I don't care that it happened when you were in college. This can't happen again."

"I don't drink anymore, but even when I was—I never attacked any of those women." Sophia admired her newly manicured nails. "At least we won't have to worry about that witch Cynthia Highcloud anymore. I heard she's not returning to the TV station. She's become a recluse."

"It was a terrible thing... what happened to her."

Sophia made a face. "I think it's a consequence of her mean-spirited actions. She wanted to hurt you, Abraham. Ruin your reputation... I will never forgive her for that. She wanted to use you to help boost her career."

"It wasn't personal, Sophia. She was just doing her job."

"Really, Abraham... how can you defend the woman who drove us to bankruptcy? She embarrassed us—the ministry..." Sophia shook her head in disbelief. "If you want to know how I really feel... Cynthia Highcloud got exactly what she deserved."

"I know exactly how you feel about her." Abraham paused in front of a mirror and began straightening his tie. "Those days are over. Our new ministry will be better than the last one. I can feel it in my spirit."

"Alright Mr. Positive."

He chuckled. "You'll see, sweetheart."

LENNI PULLED up a photograph of Abraham and Sophia

McCormick on her computer. Two years ago, Abraham was painted as the worst kind of person—one who preyed on innocent women. She just couldn't understand how Pastor Connor could choose someone like him to lead Holy Cross. Her Eli had been the associate pastor there for the past five years. He should have been the given the senior position. A man like Abraham had no business being the leader of their church.

Two weeks ago, Eli had come home announcing that he would be working under Abraham McCormick's leadership. Lenni's initial reaction was that her husband had lost his mind, but then he explained that this was an opportunity for him to learn from Abraham's charismatic personality, but to also be that shining example of how a man of God should behave.

Lenni was far from pleased with this turn of events and she made sure her husband knew how she felt. Eli should have been the senior pastor—it's what she would always believe. She'd even tried to get him to resign, but he stood firm in his decision.

She had nothing but disdain for Sophia McCormick—the woman constantly tapped her last nerve as her mother used to say. Lenni knew from the moment she met Sophia wearing a zebra-striped form-fitting dress with red patent-leather pumps that she'd be nothing but trouble.

Her attention returned to the article online.

Lenni didn't know much about Abraham, but she suspected it wasn't as innocent as he presented himself to be, although it didn't mean he was guilty of rape either. He was an extremely handsome man and a smooth talker. It was a challenge to believe that he'd had to drug anyone—just in the short time he'd been at Holy Cross, women were already throwing themselves at him whenever his wife wasn't present.

She couldn't believe how uppity Sophia acted after having

to declare bankruptcy. However, their setback proved temporary. Although Lenni couldn't stand Sophia, she did admire the woman's resilience and ability to bounce back from adversity.

"You look in deep thought."

Lenni glanced over her shoulder. "Hi hon. I didn't hear you come in."

"Why are you looking up Abraham and Sophia McCormick?"

"We need to know everything about those people."

"How would you feel if they were peeking into our past?" Eli asked. "I need you to play nice, Lenni."

"I just wanted to be reassured that we're not letting some sexual predator loose on the women in the congregation. They are our responsibility."

"I agree." He sat down in a chair facing her. "You remember when Pastor Connor went through something similar to this—he was innocent. Abraham hasn't been proven guilty of any of the charges."

"So, you think he's innocent, Eli?"

"I haven't seen anything to prove otherwise."

Lenni shrugged. "I guess we'll just have to see how this turns out."

Eli planted a kiss on her cheek. "Everything will be all right. I see God's hand all over this situation."

"If you say so. I really hope you're right."

"Are you still meeting Elizabeth for dinner?" Eli asked.

Lenni nodded.

"I won't wait up. I know how you two are when you get together—y'all talk until the sun comes up."

She gave a nervous laugh. "She's a very dear friend and we don't see each other because of her work schedule."

"Honey, I understand. Spend as much time as you want with Elizabeth. She's very nice."

Lenni kissed her husband. "Thank you. I won't wake you if it's late. I'll just sleep in the other room. I know you have to be up and out of here by four-thirty in the mornings. I'll be glad when you can quit that job and focus on ministry full-time."

"That day is on the horizon," Eli said. "We just have to be patient."

"We've been patient for five years. Joel Connor put the wrong man in charge, Eli. I know it like I know my own hand. This is going to end badly," Lenni stated. "I can feel it in my heart."

Eli was so trusting. He always chose to see the good in people—it was one of the qualities she loved about him. But she feared most it was his blind trust in others that would wound him greatly in the end.

Chapter Eleven

Abraham was as eager and erratic as a summer storm. He had an itch that needed scratching.

He loved his wife, but he had always remained true to his nature. He loved women—all women. He loved sex. Sophia was sexy, but the truth was that she just wasn't enough to satisfy his insatiable lust.

The restaurant lighting was dim, casting a warm glow around the room. Abraham's eyes traveled the room, landing on a young woman with natural curls seated at the bar. From the looks of it, she was alone.

Abraham did a slow scan of the restaurant, making sure he didn't see anyone he might possibly know. Finding it filled with strangers, he relaxed.

He looked over at the woman, his gaze falling to the honey expanse of her neck and downward.

She was watching him in the mirror behind the bar. Her gaze was a soft as a caress.

Abraham decided to make his move.

He strode up to the bar. "Is this seat empty?"

She didn't miss his obvious examination and approval. Smiling, she said, "Not anymore."

"I'm Abraham."

"Fallon. It's nice to meet you."

She had a gorgeous smile. He hadn't realized just how stunning she was up close. Her beauty literally took his breath away. The love cut of her dress showed off her beautiful full cleavage.

"What are you having?" the bartender asked.

"Sparkling water with lime," Abraham responded.

Fallon looked at him in surprise. "Water?"

"I don't drink," he responded. "Not since college."

Fallon played with her glass of wine. "So, what made you come sit here if you're not drinking?"

"I saw that you were alone and since I'm here by myself—I thought we could keep each other company."

"You don't drink anything? Not even a glass of wine?"

"Nothing."

"What happened back then to make you stop drinking?" Fallon inquired.

"I met the woman that would become my wife. She didn't like the man I'd become when I drank, so I quit."

"How did that work out for you?"

"Fine for a while," Abraham responded. "But then I cheated on her, so the marriage ended."

Fallon brushed away a lone tendril. "You're single."

He shook his head no. "I married the woman I had the affair with."

She burst into laughter. "And now you're here talking to me. Where's wifie?"

"At home." He took a sip of his sparking water, then

straightened his tie. "I might as well tell you that I'm also a pastor."

Fallon gasped.

"I know… I'm a terrible person. Trust me, I know."

Fallon took a sip of her wine. "I don't think you're terrible. I actually find it refreshing to find someone so honest. I can't count how many men lie about being single. Just tell the truth…"

"Yes, it's always best to be honest," Abraham said. "There's a high cost to lying." He glanced around. "Why don't we grab that table over there?"

"Sure."

He escorted Fallon to the table, then pulled out a chair for her.

"Wow. A real gentleman."

Every time she turned on that smile of hers, a sudden warmth swept through his body.

"So, what do you do, Fallon?"

"I'm an accountant."

"Really?"

She nodded. "I'm actually looking for a job. My former boss was nothing more than a bully. I got tired of it and told him off. He fired me."

"He sounds like a real jerk," Abraham said. "But I'd rather take another perspective. The Lord closed that door, and another is about to be opened."

She smiled. "I like that." Leaning closer to him, Fallon whispered, "My apartment isn't too far from here. That's if you're interested in continuing our conversation."

A tiny smile hit his lips. Abraham responded without hesitation, "Sure."

He followed Fallon to her place, parking his car across the street from her apartment building.

They walked inside and took the elevator to the fourth floor.

As soon as they entered her home, Abraham took Fallon in his arms without preamble.

He pulled her so close to him that she could hardly tell where her body left off and his began.

Fallon's hands slipped up behind his neck, drawing Abraham even closer.

"Kiss me," she whispered.

Abraham kissed her passionately on the lips before traveling down her neck.

Her moans of pleasure turned him on. Abraham pulled away from her long enough to remove her clothing.

Fallon undressed him before leading him into her bedroom.

They made love twice.

"All I can say is wow," she murmured. "I think you and I are going to be good friends."

Abraham slid out of bed. "I was thinking more of you being my lover."

"I like that even better."

"Another door has opened for you," Abraham stated while slipping on his pants. "How would you like to come work for me at Holy Cross? I'd much prefer having an in-house accountant than some firm handling our books."

"Are you serious?" Fallon asked, sitting up and allowing the cover to fall, giving Abraham full view of her naked breasts. "I hope you're not playing with me 'cause I need this job."

"It's yours." For a moment, he debated whether or not to get back into bed with Fallon.

"Wait a minute... what about your wife? Aren't you worried that she'll find out about us?"

"She won't from me," he stated. "Fallon, I hope you know that discretion is of the upmost importance."

"Honey, I'm good at keeping secrets."

SOPHIA PLACED a stack of files on her desk.

"You look beautiful."

She looked up as Shadow entered her office, pushing the door close.

"Hey, I didn't know you were back." Sophia kissed Shadow with barely restrained passion.

She retreated a step saying, "I've been lonely without you."

He gave her a heartrending gaze. "I missed you, too."

"While you were in Dallas, did you happen to hear any news about that reporter?"

"Nothing outside of the fact that she left Texas and returned to Oklahoma."

"Don't tell me that half-breed went back to the reservation?" Sophia burst into laughter. "I remember reading somewhere that her father was a tribal chief or something."

"It doesn't matter," Shadow said. "You don't have to worry about her. She's become a recluse from what I've been told."

"She must look hideous," Sophia stated. "Whoever drove her off the road—they wanted to do some real damage. Abraham warned her that nothing good would come out of her investigation. I bet she regrets not listening to him now. What about Bud Thomlinson?"

"He claims that he wasn't the one who shot Abraham."

"I hope you don't believe him," Sophia stated, "Because he's lying."

"You sound pretty sure of that—how do you know he did it?"

"That man has a past—a violent one." She met Shadow's gaze. "Did Bud ask about our location?"

"He didn't ask. I wouldn't have told him even if he had."

"And the civil lawsuit?"

"It's over. He called his lawyer while I was there."

Sophia smiled. "He was the last one. At least that part of this nightmare is over. That pig waited until after our bankruptcy was discharged to try and sue us."

"It's over," Shadow told her. "You and Abraham both can stop looking over your shoulder."

"Thank you." She placed a hand on his arm.

"Am I interrupting?" Lenni inquired from the doorway.

Sophia sent a sharp glare in her direction. "Didn't anyone teach you to knock when a door is closed?"

"It wasn't closed all the way," she responded.

"What do you want?"

"I have a draft of the flyers for the upcoming fundraiser. We can't move forward without your approval. That is what you said, am I correct?"

"Yes, I did say that." She leaned over and whispered to Shadow. "We'll finish our discussion later."

Shadow walked briskly past Lenni without uttering so much as a word to her.

Sophia noted the expression on her face and almost burst into laughter. Lenni had the nerve to be offended by Shadow's snub.

"You two looked pretty cozy when I walked in. I'm glad it was me and not your husband."

"Are you trying to say something, Lenni? Don't beat around the bush. *Out with it.*"

"I didn't go anywhere near a bush. I said exactly what I meant. I saw the way Shadow looked at you. I couldn't understand why he followed y'all here, but I get it now. He's here because of you. You do know he's in love with you, right?"

"I'm not going to dignify that foolishness with a response. Lenni, I'm surprised you'd be so messy. Shame on you."

She chuckled. "You're gonna have to do much better than that, *First Lady*. I know what I saw."

"This is how those sordid little rumors get started. I'm telling you now... I'd better not hear a word of this getting out, Lenni. Don't think I don't know some of your secrets—the ones you don't want anyone—especially Eli to discover. Trust me, this is not a battle you want to have with me."

Lenni's expression didn't change. She slapped the flyers down on Sophia's desk and stormed out of the office.

"Witch," Sophia uttered.

"Good news," Abraham said when Sophia entered his office a few minutes later. "Robert just called and said that Thomlinson dropped the civil suit against me."

"That's wonderful news," she said. After a brief pause, Sophia announced, "Shadow's back from his trip."

"Oh good," Abraham responded. "I need to discuss something with him."

"I hope it's about hiring more employees for security."

"That's part of it, Sophia." Just as she was about to leave, Abraham stopped her with his next sentence. "Sweetheart, I hired an accountant. She's starting on Monday."

"Why do you need a bookkeeper? We're paying Hyatt & Hyatt."

"No, Joel Connor had an agreement with them. I want someone in-house."

"Where did you find this person?" Sophia asked. "And when exactly did this interview take place? Just so you know there will be no hiring of the hoes."

"Really, Sophia? Must you be so crass? I am fully capable of making a decision on my own. I don't need your permission. You need to just act like my wife," he snapped. "I'm the one in charge of Holy Cross."

She'd never seen him act so testy. For the most part, Abraham was easygoing. He didn't like to argue and was always willing to compromise. Except on this topic apparently.

Sophia decided to let it go for now.

IT WAS OFFICIALLY over between her and Dylan.

Cynthia felt more relieved than anything else. It wasn't that she didn't love him, but she had come to realize that she was not in love with him. Since the accident, they'd spent more time apart than together. She felt she could finally close the chapter on that part of her life now.

She'd met a couple of men who expressed interest in her, but Cynthia wasn't ready to get involved with someone else. For one, she was still involved with Dylan at the time; and another, she was still working through her own issues.

Despite her parent's insistence, Cynthia still refused to see a therapist. Her desire to seek revenge was what she considered to be a universal response in her situation. It was normal to want the person to suffer for their transgressions. It wasn't an irrational desire.

Since the night of her accident, Cynthia fantasized on

ways to get even with Abraham. Sometimes she also thought of ways to get back at Gerald. It was her greatest desire to settle the score between her suffering and their actions. She had to admit that her fantasies provided her a form of sadistic pleasure but brought her no closure.

Chapter Twelve

Sophia stood up behind the enormous Art Deco desk in her office.

She stretched and yawned. It had been a long, hard day, and Sophia was beyond tired. However, the day was not over yet, because tonight she was being honored at a fabulous dinner for her charity work. As the wife of Pastor Abraham McCormick who was once again growing in popularity, Sophia was in an extremely high-profile position, so she had no choice but to accept the limelight gracefully.

She opened the middle drawer and retrieved a candy bar. Sophia hungrily nibbled on the sinfully sweet chocolate. *Nothing like a sugar rush to get me through the next few hours*, Sophia thought ruefully. Her normal workday ended at five o'clock, but because it was Wednesday, the day of their weekly Bible Study—she opted to work longer hours instead going home.

All I want to do right now is soak in my tub. Sophia closed her eyes, savoring the chocolate and the thought of a soothing bubble bath.

Outside her door, she could hear Abraham talking to one of their employees. Sophia loved the deep timbre of his voice. Whenever she thought about her husband, her face brightened. Tall, handsome and charismatic—yet, most of all, he was her soulmate, and they were truly destined to be together, but Abraham possessed one major flaw—he was unfaithful. He had an eye for the ladies.

Opening her eyes, Sophia stared up at the huge picture on the wall above the fireplace in her office. It was a formal photograph of her and two women, whom she referred to as her *ladies-in-waiting*.

Sophia smiled. Olympia and Lenni hated that reference, but she didn't care. They were married to the two associate pastors under Abraham's leadership and both were waiting for the day when their husbands would take leadership of the church.

They would have a long wait, she thought with a grin. Eli would never become pastor of this ministry. Sophia would make sure of that just because she couldn't stand Lenni Carpenter.

Olympia Robinson hadn't done anything to cross her yet. Sophia believed that the woman feared her, while Lenni seemed to thrive on creating conflict. She wasn't bothered though. Sophia sank down in her leather chair and opened the folder on her desk, as she skimmed through the photographs. She had exactly what she needed to keep Lenni under control.

She heard a feminine voice outside her office.

"Speak of the devil…," Sophia murmured to herself.

A soft knock came before Lenni stuck her head inside. "I didn't know you were still here."

"Since when am I not here for Bible Study?" Sophia asked, barely concealing her irritation.

"Oh goodness… I didn't realize it was Wednesday."

"What do you need, Lenni?"

"I wanted to talk to you about the upcoming women's day program. I think I should give the keynote."

Sophia met her gaze. "And why is that?"

"I'm a much better speaker than Olympia," Lenni responded.

Holding her hand up to stop further comment, Sophia said, "This is getting us nowhere, Lenni. I asked Olympia to speak. What's done is done."

"I thought you wanted this event to be a memorable one," Lenni said. "If you insist on

Olympia giving the keynote, it will be, but for the wrong reasons. She's long-winded and never gets to the point. Don't get me wrong… I love her like a sister, but she gets nervous and prattles on and on."

"It's going to be fine. I have everything under control."

"If you say so."

"Lenni, I realize that you're upset over the fact that my husband was given the position you wanted for Eli, but I hope that you will find a way to get over your disappointment."

"I trust Pastor Connor knew what he was doing when he chose Abraham."

"You mean *Pastor* McCormick, don't you?" How dare she not give Abraham the proper respect.

Lenni met her gaze. "I said exactly what I meant, Sophia. Your husband still has to prove that he's worthy of being *my* pastor."

Sophia's body stiffened, but she didn't respond.

"If we're done, I'm going to my husband's office. I'll see you at Bible Study." Lenni strode out of the office without another word uttered between them.

That witch thinks she's won this round.

Sophia's thoughts were interrupted by Shadow's sudden presence.

"Are you ready to leave, Mrs. McCormick?"

She smiled. "Shadow, tonight is Bible Study. I'll ride home with Abraham."

"I just wanted to check before I leave to grab something to eat."

There were times when she chose to go home instead of staying for the study, but tonight she thought it best to stay. "I appreciate your thoughtfulness."

Shadow stood near the open door, not bothering to venture closer to the desk.

A woman with a curvaceous figure paused in the hallway long enough to say, "I'm leaving for the day, First Lady…" Her eyes traveled to Shadow, lingering briefly before returning her gaze to Sophia. "I meant to tell you how pretty you look today."

"Good evening, Fallon." Sophia responded coolly, then gestured for Shadow to close the door. "I can't tell you how much I hate that little tramp," she uttered. "Did you notice the smug expression on her face? She thinks she's pulling the wool over my eyes, but I'm not stupid."

From the moment she laid eyes on Fallon Sutherland, Sophia knew that big breasted witch would soon have Abraham in her bed if she hadn't already. "I know she's after my husband."

"Are you jealous?" Shadow asked.

"No, I'm not. I just don't like that snake in the grass thinking she's getting over on me. Fallon can only do what I allow her to get away with. I hope she's smart enough to keep her emotions out of this little tryst. Abraham will never leave me."

"You seem very sure about that."

Sophia gave him a tiny smile. "I am."

"I don't understand why a woman like you puts up with a man like Abraham," Shadow stated.

"I don't expect you or anyone to understand my marriage. All I can say is that it works for me." She smiled at him. "Just like what I have with you—it works for us."

"WHEN I LEFT the office earlier, I tried to be nice to that wife of yours and she was straight up rude," Fallon complained. "She actually had Shadow shut the door in my face. I don't know why you'd want to be with a woman like that. You're too nice of a man for her. She's a witch."

"Fallon don't call her that," Abraham stated tersely. He'd stopped by for some quick loving before going back to the church to teach Bible Study. "I'm the one who's being unfaithful here. She's not stupid or blind."

"If she knows about me, then why hasn't she left you?"

"You will never understand the relationship I have with Sophia. She knows the kind of man that I am, and she loves me anyway."

"You can't really believe that she's not cheating on you. A woman who's so forgiving of your infidelity—she's got someone tickling her toes when you're not around. *Trust...*"

"Sophia is my *wife*, Fallon. I expect you to keep that in mind if you want to be in my life." Abraham removed his shirt. "We don't have much time—I have to be back at the church in about an hour."

Laughing, she said, "You're such a hypocrite."

"I am flawed…" Abraham conceded. "But I love the Lord and I know He still loves me."

Pressing her body against his, Fallon said, "I should be the one going to Jerusalem with you."

Abraham eyed her as if she'd grown another head. "Why would you think that?"

"I'm your girlfriend. Your *lover*."

"I'm not taking you on a spiritual sabbatical."

"And you're back to being hypocritical." Fallon shook her head. "I don't know why I'm wasting my time with you."

"You're not wasting time with me," Abraham said. "I care for you, but a man in my station can't parade a woman who's not his wife around in public. I thought you understood how this works—you need to play your position at all times."

"And you need to show me the same respect that you show your wife," Fallon snapped. "I'm not a whore and I won't let you treat me like one."

"That was not my intent. I'm simply stating that you are not my wife so you shouldn't expect me to treat you as if you were."

"You know what? I don't think you should come here anymore. I'm not the type of woman you want—I want to get married and have a family one day. Not spend my life as a secret lady. I look too good to be kept hidden away."

"Fallon, I'm not going to leave Sophia. I care for you, but I have too much at stake."

She shrugged in nonchalance. "That's fine. I guess it's been nice knowing you, Abraham."

He was completely blindsided by her words. "What is your problem, Fallon? Don't I treat you well?"

She nodded. "That's not the point. I want a *husband*. If you can't give me what I want, then I'm just wasting my time." She grabbed a robe from her closet and slipped it on to cover her nakedness.

"You don't want to see me anymore?" Abraham asked. "Is that what you're trying to tell me?"

"All I'm saying is that I don't want to waste time with a man who isn't interested in a future with me."

"I told you from the beginning that I wasn't going to leave my wife." Abraham had never been more confused. Fallon hadn't had a problem with his marriage until now. Maybe she was going through PMS or something, he decided.

"I didn't expect to develop feelings for you, Abraham." She met his gaze. "The sad thing about all this is that I believe you feel the same way."

"Fallon..."

"You should get back to the church," she responded. "I'm sure your wife is wondering where you are."

Abraham sighed as he buttoned up his shirt. "This isn't exactly how I thought our evening would go." He sat down on the edge of the bed to put on his shoes.

"Neither did I."

"Fallon, are you sure about this? You don't want to see me again. I enjoy spending time with you. I thought we were having a great time together. I've never seen you act this way."

"I just think it's best you leave, Abraham."

He shrugged. "If that's what you want. I'll go."

Abraham had no idea what had gotten into Fallon. He had not only considered her just a lover—she had become somewhat of a friend. He shared things with her that he'd never told Sophia. Fallon was a very good listener.

His relationship with Sophia was good, but she was a planner. Once she put something in her head—she had a one-track mind. It was all she thought about. Abraham had some ideas and plans of his own, but they often fell to the wayside. However, there was one dream that he would never let die.

Since returning to North Carolina, Abraham visited the old neighborhood in Durham where he grew up and found that the apartment building, he once lived in, was nothing more than a vacant and abandoned property.

He wanted to restore the apartments into livable space for displaced families. When he mentioned it to Sophia, she couldn't understand why he'd want to do such a thing. She felt his focus needed to be 100% on growing their ministry. He agreed with her to a certain extent, but he was never going to give up this dream. It was much too important to him.

⸻

"YOU REEK OF PERFUME," Sophia announced when Abraham returned to his office. "Go wash up. I'm assuming this is why you wanted to have a private bathroom added in here." She turned up her nose as if offended by the smell.

"It's probably yours."

"Perfumes smell differently on other women—it depends on our body chemistry. I guess you thought it was a smart move to give me and Fallon the same scent. I find it insulting."

"Sophia, you know that you're the only woman I want to spend the rest of my life with." The last thing Abraham wanted was to fight with her, especially after he'd spent the afternoon arguing with Fallon.

"You want me as your business partner," she responded. "We make a great team, so I don't have a problem with that— just don't treat me like a fool."

"I hate when you act like this."

"What? That it bothers me when you're cheating on me? Abraham, I'm long past caring about what you do as long as you're discreet. You never know who's watching."

"I have to say that's one of the things I love about you. You shoot straight from the hip."

"Wash up," Sophia stated. "There's a clean shirt in the closet. I had Olympia pick up your clothes from the cleaners."

He frowned. "Why do you treat her and Lenni like they work for you? They're married to my associate pastors. My secretary can run errands for us. Better yet, we can hire a personal assistant for you."

"Evelyn grates my nerves. Besides, Olympia was going there to pick up her husband's stuff—that's why I asked her to do it." Sophia preferred not having someone underfoot, which is why she didn't want an assistant of any kind. Instead, she enjoyed watching Olympia and Lenni

jump through hoops. She had them under her control and Sophia wasn't willing to give up the thrill of power and superiority it gave her.

"The travel agent sent over the information for our trip. I put the folder in my tote."

"I'm really looking forward to our trip to Jerusalem," Abraham said, walking out of the bathroom.

Sophia glanced up at him. "I'm assuming it will just be the *two* of us, right?" she inquired. "No Fallon... no other tramp..."

"It's just you and me. Believe it or not, I really want to spend some quality time with you, sweetheart."

She smiled. "I'd like that. I have some ideas I'd like you to consider."

"Sophia, I want us to reconnect as husband and wife."

"I want that, too."

He scanned her face. "Are you sure? I know I'm a terrible husband for the most part."

"You're a good man, Abraham. I have my flaws as well. I knew when I got with you that your ministry would be bigger than our marriage. I'm okay with that as long as you play by the rules. I won't be humiliated or made to look like a fool. I'm not Kendra."

"YOU'RE GETTING PAID good money to keep Abraham distracted. Don't lose focus, Fallon."

She admired herself in the mirror. "I'm doing my job."

"He was agitated when he left here earlier."

"I did that on purpose," Fallon responded. "I had to get him out of here—I didn't want to risk the chance of Abraham seeing you. I also don't want to make it look like I'm an easy catch—men love the chase. Besides, I didn't want you watching us while we made love."

"If you start nagging him—this relationship won't last much longer."

"I know men. Don't worry. He'll come back begging to see me. I'm giving him what he can't get from that witch of a wife of his."

"You'd better be right."

Fallon looked thoughtful for a moment.

Her phone buzzed.

"That's a text coming through from him now," Fallon said with a grin. "I told you. I got this. Now make that frown on your face disappear. Everything's going according to plan. Oh, and you might not want to keep coming around here.

Someone is bound to run into you, and it could cause questions."

"I just wanted to check things out for myself. People can tell me anything over a phone. I learned a long time ago you can't trust people."

"Why are you doing this to him?" Fallon asked.

"Stay in your lane. That's all you gotta do."

"Gandhi once said, 'an eye for an eye only ends up making the whole world blind.' He was right. Abraham isn't the man you think he is—why can't you just let this go?"

"Just do your job and keep that mouth of yours shut."

Chapter Thirteen

Cynthia slipped on a pair of linen pants and a loose, sleeveless sapphire blue top held in place by a ribbon tied around her neck. She studied her reflection in the full-length mirror. Satisfied with her clothes, Cynthia pulled her hair into a ponytail allowing a few tendrils escaping to frame her face. Her doctors had performed a miracle with the reconstruction of her facial features. There were no visible telltale scars—no one would ever know she wasn't born with this face.

No one will ever recognize me. I don't even recognize this woman staring back at me.

Cynthia released a soft sigh, then applied her make-up with a light hand. She brushed at her eyelashes with the mascara wand, then completed her look with a high-gloss lip color.

She grabbed her keys and purse.

"You're going out?" her mother asked.

"Nadine and Sabre are in town for the weekend. I'm meeting them and a few other people for dinner," Cynthia responded. "We're celebrating Bella's birthday. Do you remember her? She's Nadine's youngest sister."

"Oh okay. I think I met her a long time ago. She was in high school at the time."

"That's her. It was at her brother's wedding."

"I have to say that I'm glad to see you're starting to go out more."

"I'm taking it one day at a time, Mama."

Most of the women had already arrived by the time Cynthia strolled into the restaurant. There were going to be six of them total.

She glimpsed Sabre coming toward her and smiled.

"It's so good to see you, Cynthia. I'm so glad you decided to join us."

"Me, too." Her initial reservations vanished as she was greeted warmly by everyone.

"You're as beautiful as ever," Nadine stated. "I have to tell you I'm loving this part of Oklahoma."

"Are you thinking about relocating?"

Nadine chuckled. "No, I love my job. Unless I get an offer to relocate—I'll be in Texas."

"Do you think you'll come back to Dallas?" Sabre inquired.

"I don't think so," Cynthia responded.

They dined in a private room while drinking margaritas by the gallon.

Cynthia couldn't remember the last time she'd laughed so hard or had so much fun.

Her fingers brushed at the beads of sweat on her glass as she eyed Bella, the birthday girl who was seemingly a little drunk. Her dark curly hair spilled around her face as she sat with a lopsided grin.

She's way too happy.

Cynthia bit back a chuckle.

Nadine leaned over and whispered, "I think Bella's drunk."

"She is," she responded back. "She's enjoying herself."

Picking up her glass," Bella said, "H-Happy Birthday to me... to me." She took a sip of her margarita. "My ex-boyfriend called me earlier today under the guise of wishing me a happy birthday. Then he casually announced that he was getting married in a couple of weeks."

"How does this make you feel?" Nadine asked.

"I'm angry, but I'm not gonna let it hold me back or ruin my birthday. I'm gonna be okay."

"Yes, you will," Cynthia agreed.

Several of the other women nodded their heads in agreement.

"Let's get back to celebrating Bella," Nadine stated. "Here's to being the gorgeous and intelligent woman sitting before us. I love you, sis."

Cynthia smiled. "I concur. Bella, you're beautiful on the inside and out. I am honored to call you my friend. Happy birthday."

"My little sister is a *boss*," Nadine said between sips of margarita. "I used to be so jealous of you, Bella. You always know what to say and do in every situation. I wish I could be more like you. 'Cause if Rick had done this crap to me—I'd be in somebody's jail right now."

"I know that's right," someone uttered.

"He's not worth a prison sentence," Bella responded. "That's not to say I didn't feel that way. I learned a long time ago to love me more than I love someone else—remember, Mama used to tell us that."

After they finished eating, everyone headed to the club across the street.

Cynthia leaned against the outside wall. Taking in the fresh night air helped to clear her margarita-fogged head.

When they poured into the Carousel Night Club, the entertainment was already in full swing. Swaying to the music, Cynthia followed the rest of the women to the dance floor.

⊏⊐

ABRAHAM TOOK Sophia's hand in his as the plan soared through the air leaving Boston for Tel Aviv. He knew flying always made her nervous. To take her mind off the ten-hour flight, he said, "It's always been my dream to visit the Holy Land. My dad got the opportunity to go and I remember the profound that trip had on him. Sweetheart, we're going to be able to take what we've read in the Bible and watch it become reality."

"People kept saying that it's life-changing. That you never go home the same."

"I hope that's true," he responded. "I'd like to go back a better version of who I am now."

Sophia gave his hand a gentle squeeze. "There's nothing wrong with you, Abraham. I mean you keep certain parts of yourself under lock and key. Don't even let me get started on your womanizing tendencies… but you really have a heart for the Lord."

She stifled a yawn.

"Get some rest sweetheart."

At some point Abraham drifted off as well.

He opened his eyes and glanced out the window. A smile lit his face as he stared down at the beautiful desert sand. His father once told him that the desert was a silent witness to a holy existence.

They arrived in Jerusalem at 5 pm on Friday which was the beginning of Shabbat.

Abraham knew that Jewish businesses in the area had closed earlier in the afternoon for rest and spiritual enrichment and most would reopen on Sunday.

"We should visit the Western Wall," he suggested. "I heard it was an amazing experience."

"That's what some call the wailing wall?" Sophia asked.

"Yes. We can walk there from the hotel according to the directions."

They left twenty minutes later.

Abraham and Sophia strolled through the quiet city streets on the way to the wall. He noticed several families or groups of people, dressed up, and walking to the synagogues. As they neared the Western Wall, he saw a couple of Orthodox Jewish men wearing all black who appeared to be praying.

It was a beautiful sight to behold.

        □■□

WALKING through to Old City blew away Sophia's expectations. The ancient, narrow cobblestoned streets were lined with fruit juice stands and small shops. She felt like she was walking through a bazaar.

At the Western Wall, they had to pass through a security check.

As soon as she and Abraham entered the area, they heard chanting and praying.

Sophia glanced to her right, her gaze traveling up the hill where a group of young men were gathered, singing.

She was content with people watching, but Abraham wanted to participate. He wrote his prayer on a piece of paper and approached the Western Wall. Sophia stood beside her husband, surprised by the wave of emotion she glimpsed on his face. He had tears in his eyes as he stuck his prayer in a crack in the wall.

She was completely taken by surprise at his emotional reaction.

Abraham was strangely quiet on the way back to the hotel, so Sophia didn't push for conversation.

"Are you hungry?" she inquired.

"Not really. I'm sure you must want something. We can order room service."

"That's works. I'm beginning to feel tired. Let's just relax tonight so that we're rested up for our visit to the Holy Church."

Abraham was in complete agreement.

Later that evening, he surprised Sophia when he began undressing her.

"I love you," he whispered. "Thank you for loving me for who I am. You've never once tried to change me, and I appreciate that."

Sophia kissed him. "I love you just the way you are, Abraham."

They made love before falling asleep all snuggled together.

CYNTHIA WAS EXHAUSTED from partying until the wee hours of the morning. It had been a while since she'd stayed out so late. The morning sun poured into her windows, rousing her awake.

Her Saturday routine was down to a science; sleep in until eight, have lunch and see a movie with her mother, go grocery shopping, curl up on the couch and do some reading before going to sleep. Even though Cynthia was tired and would've preferred to sleep until noon, she didn't see any reason to change this routine.

She showered and got dressed.

"Good morning, daughter."

"Morning… I need to grab a caramel macchiato before we start our rounds," Cynthia stated. "I need the extra jolt."

"I hope you had a good time."

"I did," Cynthia responded with a smile. "It was good being out with the girls. In fact, we're going to meet Sabre and Nadine for lunch."

"Wonderful," Tracy said.

Their first stop was at a boutique.

Cynthia's attention landed on an emerald green dress hanging on one of the racks.

"Did you find something?" her mother asked.

"Not yet," she replied. "But I'm giving it some serious thought."

"That's a gorgeous color," Tracy said.

Cynthia looked over at her, their gazes connecting.

"Mama, I think I'm going to buy it. It's so cute."

"Why don't you try it on?"

She shook her head no. "I hate trying on clothes."

Cynthia ended up adding two more outfits to the dress purchase. Her mother also bought a couple of items.

They drove the short distance to the mall.

"Mama, I'm going to be broke if I go in there."

Tracy laughed. "We can just window shop—we don't have to buy anything."

"Mama, you know you can't ever walk into a store and leave empty-handed," Cynthia stated. "Neither can you."

They burst into laughter.

"It's so good to have you home."

"I thought I'd miss Dallas, but I don't. Not even a little bit."

"Do you think you'll stay in town for a while?"

Cynthia nodded. "Right now, I don't have anywhere I need to be."

"Sure, you don't want to go inside the mall?" Tracy inquired. "Macy's is having a sale."

"Okay, now you know I never turn down a sale." They exited the car and strolled into the mall.

Chapter Fourteen

The next day, Abraham and Sophia were among the crowds of visitors visiting the holy land.

She stopped to take a photograph of a man carrying a large cross as if following the path of Jesus. "This is something every Christian needs to experience."

"I think it's frowned upon to take pictures on the Shabbat."

"Oh." Sophia quickly put away her camera.

They entered the Church of the Holy Sepulchre.

Feeling a chill, Sophia rubbed her arms. *I can't believe we're standing in the spot that was once the place of the crucifixion and the tomb of Jesus.*

She twisted her mouth into a frown. Someone outside was talking and laughing loud enough for her to hear what they were saying. *It's so disrespectful,* she thought. They were on holy ground and carrying on like that.

Abraham knelt down and began to pray.

Sophia glanced around before doing the same. She was

thrilled to see the Holy Church firsthand, but she also wanted to get some shopping done. Abraham hadn't made her fully aware that they would be spending most of their time visiting churches, mosques and synagogues until this morning at breakfast. This was definitely not her idea of spending quality time together. Abraham seemed more interested in spending time with God than with her.

She immediately regretted the thought. *Please forgive me, Father God.*

———

SOPHIA AND ABRAHAM enjoyed eating dinner together at Israel's award-winning restaurant *Machneyuda*.

"You should try this spiced beef and lamb kebab," he said.

"I'm good with my vegetables and beef," Sophia responded. "Can't see myself eating lamb."

"I know there's something on your mind that you've been wanting to discuss," Abraham stated. "We might as well talk about it now. This is our last night here."

"What do you think about taping our services live for TV," Sophia said. "I always thought we should be on television. In fact, to make it more interesting, we can interview members of our audience—you know... to find out if there are any health issues. We could also collect prayer cards, Abraham. This would allow me to identify the ones you should approach."

"You mean the ones who are the most vulnerable," he stated.

"Sure."

"So how would you pass on the information to me?" Abraham asked.

"You could wear a hidden device in your ear. This way it'll look like you have a direct line to the Lord."

He nodded. "Hmmm… it could work."

"Remember how well we did with the healing cloths?"

"I don't think we want to go back down that road, Sophia."

"I'm thinking more about water. Healing water. We can send out samples," Sophia explained, "for free of course, but then after a couple of weeks—we send letters requesting a small donation of twenty dollars." She clasped her hands together. "Honey, we'd make so much money. I have a good feeling about this, Abraham. This could make us rich."

"If you're right, then I can buy my old apartment building and may even that abandoned hotel in Durham. We could turn them into homes for the homeless."

"You've been talking about this since we moved back here," Sophia said.

"That's because it's very important to me."

"So, you keep saying," she responded. "I just don't understand why. Maybe tell me that."

"It's just something I'm passionate about, sweetheart."

━━

CYNTHIA PICKED up the photo of her father that was on a nearby end table. "I used to love to watch him dance. I miss going to Pow Wows."

"There's one in two weeks," her father said from the doorway. "You should come with us."

Cynthia turned around. "When did you get home?"

"Just now. I came though the patio doors." He gestured

115

toward her mother. "Someone forgot to lock it when she left this morning."

"Mama, you can't take chances like that," she admonished. "We don't live in a safe world." A rush of anxiety washed over Cynthia as thoughts of what could've happen ran rampant in her mind.

"I'll do better," Tracy said.

"I can't believe you'd be so careless with everything that's going on—that's happened."

"Cynthia, calm down. We're all safe."

"Mama, somebody could've been in here waiting for us. From now on, I'm going to make sure all the doors and windows are locked. And that the alarm is set."

The room was enveloped in tense silence.

"You're right, Cynthia. I rushed out and I wasn't thinking. It just happened this one time, sweetie."

"I just want you and Dad to take your safety seriously. This world is an ugly place filled with horrible people."

"The world is also filled with beauty," Sam interjected. "There are still good people walking on this earth. Look at us. Are we not good people?"

Sighing softly, Cynthia said, "You know what I meant."

"What you have is a victim mentality and I'm worried about you."

"Excuse me? I was victimized twice, or did you forget?"

"Hear me out, Cynthia. I will never forget what happened to you. Don't you think it hurts me that I wasn't there to protect you? Don't you know that I would kill with my bare hands the two people who…"

Her eyes filled with tears at the anguish displayed on her father's face.

"There is a difference in being the victim of trauma and living your life with a victim mindset."

"I'm trying Dad… I'm trying hard to live a normal life, but it's not easy because I'm scared. I'm scared all the time." Cynthia broke down into sobs.

Samuel Highcloud embraced his daughter. "I understand, but you don't have to be afraid. You're safe here. Your mom and I will move heaven and earth to protect you."

Tracy handed Cynthia a tissue.

"I don't like being so negative or thinking the worse of everything and everybody." She wiped her face, then said, "I think that the only reason I feel this way now is because Abraham McCormick has disappeared. He could be anywhere and that scares me because I feel powerless. I need to find and face him, Dad. That's the only way I'll be able to move on with my life."

Chapter Fifteen

"You two look well rested from your sojourn to Israel," Eli stated when Abraham and Sophia arrived on Monday. "Welcome back."

Abraham responded. "I enjoyed our two-week sabbatical, but I'm sure glad to be home."

Lenni flicked a piece of lint off her husband's arm. "Eli and I have talked about visiting Jerusalem one day. I'm thinking we should try to go next summer."

"You should," Sophia stated. "I found the experience surreal and very spiritual." She would've preferred another day away from the church and especially Lenni, but Abraham insisted that they keep to their weekly scheduled Monday meetings.

Olympia entered the office carrying a box of pastries. "Good morning, everyone. Otis is parking the car and he'll be right in." She sat her burden down on a nearby table. "Pastor and First Lady... it's good to have you back home. We really missed y'all."

"Thank you for picking up breakfast," Sophia said. "I needed something to go with my coffee." She glimpsed the brief smirk on Lenni's face before it disappeared but pretended not to notice. "We had an amazing time, Olympia. In fact, while we were there, God gave us a special assignment."

"Oh really?"

"Abraham will tell you more about it when your husband gets here."

"Here I am," Otis said, walking briskly into the conference room.

Five minutes later, the meeting was underway.

"I had a dream the night before we left for Jerusalem. I saw people getting delivered from the power of evil spirits; saw them getting healed...then I saw water," Abraham said. "I had no idea what it meant. It wasn't until out last night there that God revealed everything to me."

"God gave him specific instructions on how to make holy water and that we are to send it to people all over the world. They can drink or sprinkle it, depending on their needs."

"Do we have to send it to a priest to have it blessed?" Lenni uttered with a chuckle.

Sophie sent a sharp glare in her direction.

"My wife grew up Catholic," Eli explained.

"We will pray over the water before we send them out," Abraham stated. "The Lord told me to call it anointed water."

"I like that," Otis stated.

Olympia nodded in agreement.

Sophia's gaze traveled around the table. Lenni and Eli sat with their expressions blank.

After a long pause, Abraham announced. "I intend to have

everything set up to move forward with the production of Anointed Water. I want to roll it out in 60 days."

"We're looking into televising our services as well. Abraham has a meeting at the end of the week with the Inspiration network."

Olympia clapped her hands in glee. "Praise the Lord," she murmured. "He's truly expanding Holy Cross's territory."

Lenni glanced over at her husband, whose expression remained unreadable.

Sophia eyed the two of them for a moment before turning her attention back to Abraham, who outlined the tasks ahead of them in preparation for the launch of Anointed Water.

Her gaze traveled over to Lenni and Eli once more. The more she watched them, the more her irritation grew. She thought of the information in her desk on Lenni. Sophia knew the time would come when she'd have to play her hand. She was determined to keep Lenni under her thumb. Abraham liked Eli, but Sophia wasn't sure how Eli felt about her husband. He appeared loyal, but with Lenni in his ear...

⊏▭⊐

"ELI and I will not be a party to whatever scheme you and Abraham have come up with," Lenni stated as she entered Sophia's office without knocking. "Sending people packets of water? You can't be *serious*."

Irked, Sophia stated, "I'm busy."

"You may want to take time for this," Lenni responded. "I know all about what happened in Texas."

Sophia met her gaze. "*And...*" She was in no way intimidated by this woman. What she felt was mere irritation for the interruption.

"I'm sure you don't want a repeat of what must have been a dreadful time for you and Abraham."

"Let me make sure I understand what's going on right now." Sophia sat up straight in her chair. "Are you threatening me?"

"I'm simply reminding you of what happened the last time you and your husband tried to defraud your members. Not to mention all those women who came forward accusing him of rape."

"You know you shouldn't believe everything you read in the newspaper. If you'd done your research, you'd know that Abraham was cleared of any wrongdoing where those women are concerned."

Lenni gave a short laugh. "So, you're saying that it's what? *Fake news?*"

"Why don't we talk about you, Lenni?"

Arms folded across her chest, she asked, "What about me?"

"Is your husband accepting of your female lovers?"

Shocked, Lenni's mouth dropped open, but no words came out. She had no idea how Sophia had found out but with this information—she was dangerous.

"Personally, I could care less who you choose to have an affair with, but since you made the mistake of confronting me..."

Lenni was not about to admit the truth. Instead, she said, "I'm sorry but I don't know what you're talking about."

"You and Elizabeth Storm were roommates in college. I suspect you two have been lovers all this time. What I don't understand is why you both stayed in the closet. The world today is more tolerant of same sex relationships."

"Elizabeth and I are friends, Sophia. Nothing more. I can't

believe you're sitting here trying to insinuate otherwise. We're simply close friends."

"I agree that you're very close." She opened the folder on her desk and pushed a photograph toward Lenni. "This is a judgement-free zone. Let's just talk." Sophia gestured toward an empty chair. "Sit down."

Taking a seat, Lenni avoided looking at the photograph. "How did you get that picture? Have you been spying on us?"

"I wanted to know who I was dealing with, so I did a little research—same as you," Sophia stated.

"Eli doesn't know about my relationship with Elizabeth. I want to keep it that way."

"Well, this will depend on how well you and I work together."

Lenni wiped away her tears. "You're blackmailing me."

"Look, I don't want to tear apart what you have with Eli."

"Then what do you want?"

"I want you to mind your own business and stay out of the church affairs. You also need to keep your husband under control. You do this and your secret will remain safe with me."

"How do I know I can trust you?"

"Lenni, I could've outed you a long time ago," Sophia said. "I've known about your little secret for a while."

"When did you find out?"

Sophia waved her hand in dismissal. "It doesn't really matter, does it?"

Lenni rose to her feet. "Are you finished?"

"Do we have an agreement?"

"I don't have any other choice," Lenni murmured. "I wish I could say that your actions surprised me, but it doesn't."

"You can leave my office now."

"Perfectly fine with me," Lenni responded. "I can't get out of here fast enough."

She left the church and drove straight to the Brier Creek area where Elizabeth lived. She needed to warn her friend.

Lenni sat in her car for a few minutes summoning up the courage to ring the doorbell. She hated bringing drama to Elizabeth, but she had no choice. She couldn't sit back and let her be blindsided should Sophia decide to make good on her threat.

Elizabeth opened the door just as she reached the top step.

"Lenni, what are you doing here?" Elizabeth glanced over her shoulder. "Wiley is home…"

Keeping her voice low, Lenni said, "I'm sorry. I had to come tell you that we have to end things. Sophia knows about us."

"What? *How?*"

"I don't know," Lenni responded. "We will both lose everything if she opens her mouth. Elizabeth, I can't let that happen."

"I told you she was not to be trusted."

"I know and you were right. I never cared for Sophia, but I thought the woman had some morals."

"Lenni, what does she want from you?"

"Sophia wants me under her thumb." She released a soft sigh. "It's not your problem. I'll have to figure this out."

"Are you sure you can keep her quiet?"

"I'll find a way." Lenni paused a heartbeat, then said, "Goodbye Elizabeth."

Back in the car, she wiped away her tears and headed home.

She was surprised to find Eli there.

"I thought you'd still be at the church," she told him.

"What do you think about this idea of Abraham's?" Eli asked.

Lenni chose her words carefully. "It's something worth pursuing, I guess."

"Really? I thought you'd be completely against it."

"Why would you say that?"

"Well, because you and I both know there is no special power of God in this anointed water any more than there is in the oil in which the ancients of Israel were anointed."

"You're right," Lenni responded. "We know that it's the Spirit of God who performs extraordinary miracles through the hands of the ministry. Most people may not realize it, so we have make sure it's clear to all who receive those packets of water."

Eli nodded in agreement. "I guess the problem I have with this is that God's power is not in oil or water... yet we pray over oil and we anoint people. When Timothy was suffering with stomach problems and other infirmities and Epaphroditus was sick to the point of death, Paul never once offered to send oil to them. Timothy was encouraged to drink some wine."

"Well, I can see using oil to anoint the sick," Lenni said, "because James 5:14 says, is anyone among you sick? Let him call for the elders of the church, and let them pray over him, anointing him with oil in the name of the Lord."

"Like you said, we just have to make sure people understand that these water packets are symbolic—they have no special power." Eli sat down beside her. "What's wrong, sweetheart? I can tell something's weighing on you heavily."

"I'm just tired. I think I'm going to go up and take a nap."

"I'll probably head back to the church in an hour or so," Eli said. "You want me to wake you up? We can ride together."

"No," she responded. "I'm not going back there—not today anyway."

Lenni waited until Eli left home to fall on her knees to ask God for His forgiveness.

"Father God, please forgive me of my sins. I repent of them all and ask to be washed clean as snow. Please help me to be a good and faithful wife to my husband. Close my eyes to any person outside my marriage who may tempt me to stray. I love Eli—the man You blessed me with, and I don't want to lose him. Father, I know I've wronged him, but please give me the chance to do better. In Jesus' precious name I pray. Amen."

ABRAHAM STARED at the photo of Fallon in his phone. A part of him wanted to see her, but he was not about to let Fallon believe that he would come running after her every time she had a tantrum.

Outside of the office, he hadn't seen or spoken to her in a couple of weeks.

He needed to vent so he went to talk to Shadow.

"What can I do for you, Abraham?"

"I have a situation with Fallon."

Shadow leaned back in his chair. "Is she becoming a problem?"

"No, it's nothing like that. We just aren't seeing eye to eye. She wants more than I can give her."

"I love Sophia. I just want Fallon to stay in her role. She's good at her job, but there doesn't need to be any tension, especially here at the church. The last thing I need is drama. I've had enough to last a lifetime."

"I assume you told her all this."

Abraham nodded. "She broke things off with me. It's just that she's bringing it to work with her. I spoke to her this morning in the break room and she just walked out like I hadn't said a word."

"Maybe you should let her go," Shadow suggested. "Problem solved."

"If I can be honest, the truth is that I can't get Fallon out of my mind. I enjoy her company. I miss our friendship."

"It sounds like you may care more about this girl than you realize."

Shadow's words gave Abraham pause for thought.

Chapter Sixteen

Cynthia sat on the edge of her bed in her pajamas, her hand holding the remote. The glow of the television was the room's only light. She surfed through channels when she happened upon the Inspiration network.

Shockwaves crashed over her as she watched Abraham McCormick standing in a pulpit preaching to a full audience. He hadn't changed much, except for a few wrinkles under his eyes.

He was as mesmerizing as ever.

Seated on the stage in an upholstered chair, Sophia sat there watching her husband, a smile plastered on her perfectly made-up face. Cynthia focused in on Abraham who implored his TV audience to call an 800 number. "Call now for your free packet of Anointed Water."

"Anointed water," Cynthia repeated. "What in the world…"

As if to answer the question that occurred to her, Abraham said, "I can see the Lord changing the lives of His people. I see

Him leading people into new houses and cars. I see Him cancelling debts. I see supernatural healing... I'd like to send you the Anointed Water."

He walked down the steps stopping near a woman with a cane. "I believe the Lord's given you a divine healing. You can now walk without the cane."

Abraham extended his hand to her. "Stand up and walk. We need to make the enemy mad."

The woman stood up, with his help; her hands shaking, she took a step. Then another. Tears streaming down her face, she took another step.

Abraham picked up the cane and tossed it onstage.

Cynthia noticed that while she didn't take many more steps, she seemed to come alive, vibrating with energy. She began to praise the Lord for healing. "I put that anointed water in my shoes every night. I even put some on my daughter's pillow." She turned and pointed. "She's here with me today. She came to give her life to Christ. Praise the Lord of Lords—my Heavenly Father. Praise Him..."

"Is he crying?" she muttered.

The camera zoomed in on Abraham, his eyes tear bright. He embraced the woman, then gestured for her daughter to join them. The audience was up on their feet, filling the air with shouts of Hallelujah and praises to God.

Cynthia continued to watch Abraham moving around the congregation, hugging people; pausing every now and then to pray with some.

He made his way back to the pulpit and said, "I've heard testimony after testimony. Addictions gone, healing, people being saved. Strongsholds sent back to the pits of hell. Give the Lord some praise right now. He deserves your praise. You not praising me—I didn't do it." Abraham pointed upward. "This is all *Him*."

Cynthia stared at the TV, transfixed. Abraham was resurrected. Back in Dallas, he was becoming one of Dallas's more popular televangelists when Nadine and the other women brought the charges against him. She still believed that he paid off some of his accusers, while the others were conveniently caught in an outright lie or dates didn't add up. She knew Nadine was telling the truth, but her friend just wasn't up to what would surely be a long and intense court battle.

Back then, Abraham would call out a name and ailment of someone in the audience that he'd never met. Cynthia figured he wanted it to appear as if God had given him the information. In his arrogance, he dared people to doubt his God-given ability to make these divine revelations.

He never gives up, I see.

Neither do I.

Cynthia wasn't convinced that the woman and her daughter were nothing more than props to motivate the television audience to order Anointed Water.

"I love sharing the reality of God's saving power; His healing power… His debt cancelling power. I am a testimony of how God can transform a life of poverty to one of affluence. *Amen?*"

"Amen," the audience responded in unison.

She had the presence of mind to write down the phone number.

"You won't get away this time. I'm going to prove to the world that you are nothing but a fraud."

THE NEXT MORNING, Cynthia called the number. She got a recording asking her name and the address to send the Anointed Water. "This is Angela Ray. I would like to receive the Anointed Water. My address is PO Box 67, Tahlequah, Oklahoma. Zip code is 74464."

"What was that all about?" her father inquired when she hung up. She'd had no idea that he had entered the family room. "Anointed Water?"

"McCormick has resurfaced. He's in North Carolina peddling something he calls Anointed Water. I want to find out more about it."

"He doesn't give up... I'll say that."

"There were people on television giving testimonials of how this is more of a miracle water. Dad, they really believe they were actually healed—some say it got rid of evil spirits and others said that they received money. It's nothing but a scam and I'm going to prove it."

"You aren't a reporter anymore."

"I may not work for a news station, but I can make sure that the world knows what kind of man McCormick is—he's a terrible, fraudulent man—one who rapes women."

"You're going after him."

Cynthia eyed her father. "Yes, I am. Dad, I have to do this for Nadine and all of the other women this man attacked. Now he's come up with another way to take advantage of people."

"Do you have a plan?"

She smiled. "Yes, and I could really use your help. Abraham McCormick can't see me coming after him.

"MORE AND MORE CALLS ARE COMING IN for the Anointed Water. This is more than I could've ever imagined."

"I knew this would work," Sophia told Abraham as they settled down to eat dinner. "We're going to be rich, babe."

"It's not really about wealth for me. I want to achieve my dream of providing homes for the homeless."

"You're still thinking about that?"

"Of course," he responded. "I can't stand seeing homeless people sleeping on the streets like that."

Abraham was caught up in memories of his past.

"What are you thinking about?" Sophia asked. She hated whenever he stared off into space—it was like he was in another place and time. There were times when his eyes were bright with unshed tears.

"It's nothing," he responded. "I'm just trying to figure out my next move."

"Abraham… you know you can tell me anything, don't you? There shouldn't be any secrets between us." Sophia paused a moment, then said, "I already know about your infidelities. It can't get any worse than that."

"Why do you put up with me?"

"I love you, Abraham," Sophia answered. "We make a great team. I know the type of man you are. I know that you love me. If you didn't—I would've walked away a long time ago."

"You're right. I love you more than my own life, Sophia. I don't deserve you, but I'm so grateful to have you in my life. You understand me and my needs."

"I wouldn't go that far," she responded. "I don't understand why I'm not enough woman for you. I don't understand why you don't have a faithful bone in your body. I'm just tolerant. For now, anyway." She took a sip of iced water.

"You are the only woman for me, Sophia."

"Try remembering that when you're lusting at another woman. Another thing... leave it outside the doors of our church. I won't have you humiliating me in front of our members. I know you're sleeping with Fallon. I've known for a while."

Abraham looked surprised but recovered quickly.

"I keep telling you I'm not stupid. If you want to see that tramp—she has to leave the church. In fact, I want her gone already. If you don't fire her—*I will*."

"She's good at her job, Sophia. We have to have someone we can trust in that position. We have a lot of money coming in."

"And you think your mistress should be watching over it? What happens when things sour between you two? You don't think she'll carve out a nice little nest egg for herself?" She looked Abraham in the eye. "How do you know that she hasn't been stealing from us?"

"I know because I have cameras all over that room and a key logger on her computer—every computer in that room, in fact."

"Good to know that you're still thinking with your brain when it comes to our money. However, I still want her fired."

"I'll take care of it."

"*Tomorrow*," Sophia stated. "I don't want to see Fallon's face in the building."

"I said I'll take care of the situation."

Did he just sound like he had an attitude? She eyed her husband. *Was he falling in love with Fallon?* Sophia had never seen him react this way about another woman. Oh yeah, Fallon definitely had to go.

⊏⊐

FALLON LOOKED up from her computer when Abraham entered the office but didn't speak.

"Good morning," he greeted.

Silence.

He was glad none of the others in her department had arrived. He needed to make this quick. "The reason I came here is to tell you that I have to let you go."

She glared at him. "Excuse me? Oh, so I don't speak to you and I get fired. Is that how you do people you claim to care about? I know I've had an attitude with you, but it's got nothing to do with my job. I'm sorry."

"That isn't why, Fallon."

"Then why?" she demanded. "I do my work."

"The reason you can't work here is because it upsets my wife."

Her eyes filled with tears. "You can't just fire me, Abraham. You know my situation. I need to have a job."

"Look, you can keep your salary. Sophia doesn't want you in the building and I have to respect her wishes. She knows that I'm sleeping with you, Fallon. But not only that... you got other people around here talking because of the attitude you've had with me. I'm your boss—you can't go around just ignoring me."

"So, you want me to work from home?"

"No," Abraham responded. "But you'll stay on our payroll —I feel bad for placing you in this position."

She gasped in surprise. "My full salary?"

"Yes."

"What will your wife have to say about that?"

"She won't know," he responded. "This is just between you

and me."

"I guess I'd better pack up my stuff then," Fallon said. "I have to say that this is probably the easiest money I've ever made."

"I'm sorry."

She smiled. "I'm actually okay with it. Just make sure I get my checks every payday. I have bills to pay. I hope we're not over because I do miss you."

Just as Abraham opened his mouth to respond, Sophia strode into the office asking, "Why is *she* still here?"

"He just informed me that my services were no longer needed," Fallon stated. "I'm about to pack up and leave. I don't want to be where I'm not wanted."

"That's good to hear," Sophia responded. "Have Shadow check her bags and escort her to her car."

"That's not necessary," Abraham stated.

"Yes, it is," she countered. "Best of luck to you, Fallon." She paused on her way out to tell her husband, "We have a meeting in twenty minutes."

"Why do you let her talk to you this way?"

"Sophia has always been very direct. It's one of the qualities I love about her."

"You're the one who has to live with her, so it's not my problem." Fallon pushed away from her desk. "I'm direct as well, but not to the point of rudeness. There's a difference."

Abraham checked his phone. "I should be able to leave here around 6:30 or 7 tonight. I'd love to spend time with you. I haven't been able to get you out of my mind."

"Does this include dinner?" Fallon asked.

He grinned. "And *dessert*."

"I'll see you tonight. You better get to your meeting before First Lady Sophia comes looking for you."

Chapter Seventeen

A few days later, Cynthia received a letter from McCormick with a clear packet of liquid along with detailed instructions on how to rid her home of evil spirits by sprinkling the water on the doorways. She was to drink the water to cure her of any illnesses and if seeking a financial blessing.

"Oh yeah... *Pastor* Abraham McCormick is definitely back to his old tricks," she murmured while examining the sachet of water. In Dallas, his church sent out fabric squares they called healing cloths. "Some people just don't learn."

The one thing that puzzled her was the fact that there wasn't a monetary request. Cynthia was pretty sure that he had to be making money off this scheme of his somehow.

Her suspicions were confirmed when she received a second letter four days later asking for $20 to be sent to plant the seed.

"Did you drink that anointed water?" her father asked.

She burst into laughter. "You know I'm not going to drink whatever is in that packet. I don't need a blessing from McCormick. He actually wants me to send the little bag back to him. He probably recycles them. I just got another letter asking for $20 to plant a seed. I told you that man is a fraud."

"Here's everything you need."

Cynthia embraced her father. "Thank you, Dad. I know you hated going to your cousin like this, but I appreciate it. I promise you it won't be in vain."

"Just be careful."

"I will, Dad. I love you."

"I love you, too Cynthia."

"You better get used to calling me Phoenix."

"You know your mother isn't too happy about this decision."

She nodded. "I have to do this—not just for Nadine, but for me as well. I won't be able to fully move on with my life until this is over."

"There's a credit card in there for emergencies. If you find yourself in danger, don't hesitate to use it."

"Thank you again for everything."

"You're my daughter. I'd do anything for you. If you need me to come to North Carolina… I'm there."

⬛

ABRAHAM READ the letter then placed it back into the envelope.

He picked up his phone. "Shadow, I need you to come to my office immediately."

"I'll be right there. I'm next door."

Seconds later, Shadow entered Abraham's office, asking, "Is everything okay?"

"I got this today." He held out the letter.

You think you can do your dirt and get away with it? Well, you can't, preacher man. Hiding behind the Bible won't save you. I'm coming for you.

"Do you think this could be the same person who shot me?" Abraham asked after Shadow read the contents.

"Could be," was his response.

"I guess this person found me because of the commercials. I really thought that part of my life was over with; especially since I was cleared of the rape charges." He rubbed his chin. "I don't have any idea who would want me dead."

"If I may speak candidly..." When Abraham nodded, Shadow continued. "Have you considered that it could be a boyfriend or husband of one of the women you've dealt with —some men don't handle that sort of thing well."

"There's only been one woman that was married. I never met Maisie's husband. You think it could be him? I do know he was in the military."

"Anything's possible," Shadow stated. "I can run a background check on him—see what he's been up to, if you'd like."

"Of course," Abraham responded. "We need to find out who's trying to kill me."

Shadow turned to leave.

"Oh, and please don't mention this to my wife. I don't want Sophia to worry."

"What if they decide to go after her?" Shadow inquired. "Your wife needs to be protected as well."

"You're right of course. I don't want anything to happen to Sophia. I need you to keep her safe. I want you to be with her at all times. I only trust you."

"I can do that. I'll have Eugene and Rodrick accompany you. We have to take this threat seriously."

"Can they be trusted?"

Shadow nodded. "I vetted them myself. They know to be discreet when it comes to sensitive situations."

———

A WEEK LATER, Cynthia stepped off the plane at the Raleigh-Durham Airport in North Carolina. Armed with her new identity, she was ready to take on Abraham McCormick, but first, she had to find a place to live.

She was met in the Baggage Claim area by a realtor who was going to take her to look at potential housing.

By the next day, she'd already decided on a place to live. She left her hotel and took an Uber to the real estate office to sign off on her paperwork.

"Miss D'Angelo, you're all set."

"Thank you and please... call me Phoenix."

Later that afternoon, she settled in her room at the Aloft hotel. She turned on her computer and searched the job openings at McCormick's church. Phoenix broke into a smile when she saw the position in the accounting department. "This is perfect."

She had a resume already prepared and uploaded it. Phoenix was grateful for her father's help in setting up her new identity. There was no way for Abraham McCormick to connect her alias back to Cynthia Highcloud.

"I really need to get this job," she whispered. It was the only way to know just how much money McCormick was bringing from this scam, but not only that—she would learn all the inner workings, making it easier for her to topple his industry.

Chapter Eighteen

Phoenix strolled into Holy Cross Healing & Deliverance Ministries with an ease she displayed but did not feel. The facility was huge, much bigger than the church Abraham had in Dallas. She eyed the stunning artwork that adorned the walls in the common area.

She walked up to the reception area and was greeted warmly by a young woman. "Good afternoon Ms..."

"D'Angelo. Phoenix D'Angelo," she said smoothly. "I'm here for an interview."

"Yes, of course. You're here for the accounting position. You'll be interviewing with Pastor McCormick."

"Wonderful," she murmured.

Phoenix sat down in one of the visitor chairs, and quietly observed the people roaming about. From what she could tell, the environment was warm and friendly. She heard lots of laughter in the hallways.

Out the corner of her eye, she caught sight of Sophia

McCormick with two other women. They walked into one of the conference rooms, closing the door behind them.

Abraham appeared from around a corner dressed in an expensive-looking suit, exuding his friendly and easygoing personality.

"Miss D'Angelo, it's very nice to meet you," he greeted with a warm and welcoming smile. "I was just going over your resume. Very impressive."

They walked into a huge corner office.

Abraham navigated around an exquisite designed oak desk. "Please make yourself comfortable."

She sat down in a chair facing him. "Thank you for the opportunity to interview for this position."

Abraham eyed her for a moment before saying, "As I mentioned earlier, I am very impressed by your resume."

Phoenix searched his eyes for a flicker of recognition but found none. She settled back in the visitor's chair across from his desk.

"I see you relocated here from New Orleans. What brought you to North Carolina?"

"I was looking for a place to start over," Phoenix responded. "I broke up with my boyfriend of five years and wanted a new beginning. I have a friend here and she said this was the place for that. So here I am."

"Your friend's right," Abraham said. "This is home for me. My wife and I moved back here a couple of years ago. We came here for a fresh start as well."

His questions were well thought out and designed to evoke a full response. Not one-worded answers. Phoenix never once felt violated by his gaze or that he was focused on any of her assets. Adam was professional throughout the entire interview.

She was a bit surprised by this, however. After all, he was a sexual predator.

At the end, Phoenix commented, "I've been hearing so much about this Anointed Water.

I have to say I've never heard anything like this."

"God has truly blessed us," Abraham said. "He planted it in my heart while my wife and I were in Jerusalem."

"All the stories I've heard make it sound like it's something magical."

Abraham shook his head in denial. "Anointed Water is what I'd call a Biblical connection. There's nothing magical or mystical about it. Those testimonies are real."

"Biblical connection?"

"Yes. The Bible uses connections like this to release miracles. I can't tell you the number of people who have used Anointed Water and their lives changed."

"That's really wonderful," Phoenix murmured, feigning an excitement she didn't feel.

"What is your relationship with the Lord?"

"Fragile, at best," she responded. Phoenix decided the truth was the best way to go in this situation. "I have to be honest, Pastor McCormick. I wasn't raised in the church. I believe in the one God but haven't really pursued a real relationship with Him. I want to change that, but it's not been easy."

"I understand. There was a time I was in your shoes. But one day I found myself in a situation that only the Lord could bring me out. The difference between us is that I was raised by parents in ministry. Still, I felt so far away from God."

"And now you're following in your father's footsteps."

Abraham nodded. "He knew this day would come—my

dad. I was thirteen when he told me that I would one day preach the Word. I remember laughing."

"I suppose he has the last laugh now," Phoenix stated.

"Welcome to Holy Cross Healing & Deliverance Ministries, Miss D'Angelo." His eyes were tender, and his smile genuine. "I hope you will accept this position. I feel deep in my spirit that you're the perfect person for this job."

She forced a smile. "I won't disappoint you. I appreciate the opportunity."

Abraham gave her a tour of the administrative building and the church. "I would love for you to attend Sunday services with us."

"I assumed it was a requirement for job."

"I would say it's highly recommended. However, members of my staff will tell you that it is a requirement."

Abraham was nothing like she'd imagined. He wasn't arrogant and personable. His warmth didn't appear to be fake—he seemed very genuine, in fact. However, maybe he was just a great actor.

Phoenix refused to let her guard down. Abraham McCormick could not be trusted.

"WHO WAS that woman I saw you with?" Sophia inquired when she entered her husband's office.

"She's our new accountant. You had me fire Fallon, remember?"

Arms folded, she uttered, "Oh *really*? I thought we'd decided that I would be the one to do the hiring from now on. Let me see her resume."

Abraham handed the paper to his wife.

"She seems more than qualified. Did you verify Miss D'Angelo's references?"

"I did. She came with glowing recommendations."

"I didn't get a real good look at her, but she does remind me of someone…" Sophia said. "I just can't put my finger on who." She glanced down at the paper. "It says that she's from New Orleans. How did she come to be here in North Carolina?"

"She came here for a new beginning. She ended a long-term relationship and just wants a fresh start."

Sophia broke into a grin. "Oh wow. So that's why you gave her the job. She's heartbroken and you want to make it all better."

"She's not my type and you know that."

"One word of advice, husband… stay away from the help or any of the members. I mean it."

Abraham changed the subject by asking, "Have you seen Shadow?"

"He's in the training room. He has two new members on his team. You told him we needed more security, *remember*? What I'd like to know is why?" Sophia eyed her husband. "Is there something going on I should know about?"

"Our church is growing, and we've got a lot of money coming in on a daily basis," Abraham stated. "I would rather err on the side of caution."

Sophia seemed satisfied with his response. "Well, going forward, I will do the interviewing and hiring around here. I can be a little more objective."

"That's fine with me," Abraham said. "I received a phone call from Mark Watson in Maryland. He wants me to be the guest pastor for his church anniversary. Do you want to go with me?"

Sophia shook her head. "You know I can't stand to be around that long-winded man. On top of that, he thinks he knows everything. I think I should just stay here and look after things."

"You have Lenni and Olympia... they'll be here."

"I'm not about to leave them in charge of anything," she stated. "Especially over the money. I don't trust anybody when it comes to the cash coming in."

"Sweetheart, we have security."

"I know all that, Abraham. I don't care about cameras, key loggers—none of that. If I had the time to count all the money myself... trust me, I would. People are greedy. They will steal us blind if we're careless."

"I'll leave Shadow here."

She smiled. "Great. I trust him. I don't feel as comfortable with Marcus or those other guys."

"We have a good team of men, Sophia. You just have to get to know them."

"I know," she responded. "It took me a while to get used to Shadow, remember?"

Abraham placed a hand to her back. "What do you think about leaving here in about an hour? We can play hooky for the rest of the day."

"Are you serious?"

"Yes, I want to spend some quality time with my wife, if she's interested."

"I can assure you she's very interested," Sophia responded. She placed a kiss on Abraham's lips, then slipped out of her dress.

"Here?"

"It's not like we're in the sanctuary. This is your office.

C'mon… let's be spontaneous," she locked the door, then led him over to the leather sofa.

Their passion spent, the washed off quickly in the bathroom.

When Sophia opened the door to leave, she found Lenni standing in the hallway.

"Were you looking for me?"

"I was." Pointing to her hair, Lenni said, "You might want to run a comb through your hair. You've got a case of bed head."

Sophia grinned. "You're looking a little jealous."

She stiffened. "The new youth books are in your office."

"Thank you."

Lenni brushed past her without uttering a response.

Abraham appeared in the doorway.

"Some people are super sensitive," Sophia said.

"Sweetheart, go comb your hair."

"I'll take care of it when I get to my office. My comb is in my purse. All it shows is that the pastor and his first lady are still very passionate people."

Later that evening, they sat at home laughing about the rumors of their lovemaking made its way around the administrative building.

"At least this time I'm the wife and not the mistress," Sophia said.

"True."

She studied his face. "I've known you a long time, Abraham."

He smiled. "Since we were in the ninth grade. Back then, I never thought I'd have a chance with you."

"You were cute but very shy. You didn't know how to talk

to a girl. When we reconnected years later—you were a completely different person."

"Kendra had a lot to do with that," Abraham stated. "She was my first friend in college. She was a nice person."

"Yet you cheated on her with me."

"I did."

"Do you regret it?"

"What I regret is hurting a woman who didn't deserve it, Sophia."

"Do you ever wonder if that's why we've had so many problems with trying to have a baby? Maybe it's a consequence of our actions. I pretended to be Kendra's friend only for access to you. I wanted you and I wasn't about to let anyone stop me, including your wife." Sophia put a hand to his face. "I was the one who sent those pictures of us making love to her."

"Why did you lie when I asked you about it all those years ago?"

"Because I thought you'd leave me and go back to her. If Kendra wasn't happily married to someone else—I might not be telling you this now."

"Why did you decide to come clean?"

"I don't want there to be any secrets between us, Abraham."

"I know," he responded.

"One more thing. When you go to Maryland tomorrow, do me a favor and keep Fallon out of sight. Side chicks are only to be seen and heard in the bedroom. Remember that, Abraham."

"COME BACK TO BED..." Sophia cooed.

"I won't be long."

She eyed his tall muscular frame. "You are truly a very sexy man, Shadow."

He smiled. "We always have a good time together, but you know we can't keep doing this. Abraham is bound to find out."

Sophia sat up in bed, pulling the covers up to hide her nakedness. "He won't. Abraham would never believe that I'd cheat on him."

"You may believe that, but I also know you don't want him to ever find out."

She stretched. "The way you make me feel when we make love... I don't care if I ever lay eyes on Abraham again."

Shadow chuckled. "Now I know you're lying. You've made it clear that you will never leave your husband."

"The only thing that would make me leave him is if he gets someone pregnant. That would be the ultimate betrayal." Sophia clasped her hands together. "Abraham and I have tried for ten years to have a baby. We tried everything... I can't bear the idea of another woman carrying his child. It would destroy me."

"Why don't we change the subject to something more pleasant," Shadow suggested.

"Why talk at all?" Sophia responded.

Chapter Nineteen

"You need any help with your boxes?"

Phoenix glanced over her shoulder to find a very handsome man standing on the sidewalk carrying a bag of groceries.

"Thank you, but no... I'm good."

"I'm Julian Nelson. I live next door."

"Nice to meet you," she responded. "I'm Phoenix D'Angelo."

"*Phoenix*. I like that." He sat the bag in a wicker chair on his porch. "Let me help you get this stuff inside. It will take half the time if we work together."

"What about your food?"

"There's nothing in there that will spoil."

"Thank you, Julian."

He was right. They were done an hour later.

Relief swept over her when Julian didn't try to make up an excuse to hang around after everything was in the house. She didn't even have to ask him to leave.

"I hope you enjoy your stay here, Phoenix. This is a pretty quiet neighborhood. Good families."

She walked him to the door. "It's already beginning to feel like home."

———

MONDAY MORNING, Phoenix arrived for her first day at Holy Cross where she was greeted by Sophia. "Good morning. Abraham told me you'd be starting today. I'm Sophia McCormick.

Everyone here addresses me as First Lady or First Lady Sophia."

"It's nice to meet you."

She followed Sophia to the accounting office. "This is where you'll be working."

"Can I ask you a question?" Phoenix asked.

Pausing in the doorway, Sophia questioned, "What is it?"

"The Anointed Water… where does it come from?"

"Why do you ask?"

"Because I read somewhere about a spring in Southern Russian that is supposed to have magical healing properties."

"Our water comes from Jerusalem. Our prayer ministry leaders pray over the packets before we send them out of love, faith and obedience."

"And they send you money in return."

"In the form of a donation," Sophia stated. "It's purely voluntary."

Right, Phoenix thought. The last time she talked to her father, several letters had arrived asking for money.

———

"WHY ARE you writing these letters, Eli? Lenni asked. She picked up one and read aloud:

"I speak to you now as a messenger of the Lord… I plead with you to avoid making the mistakes of others and allow shortage or adversities to affect your generosity. Do not think of the things you need…. For if you give, I will supply all your needs."

She tossed it into a nearby trash can. "Really? How can you agree with this… this thing that Abraham's doing?"

"We tell people this same thing every Sunday," Eli responded. "If they are benefiting from the ministry, why not ask them to sow into it?"

"Lenni, these letters work. Most people send more than the $20 we ask."

"I guess you forgot about the one that came back with a bag of dog poop."

"We can't please everyone."

"We shouldn't be a part of this, Eli. I'm telling you—we're going to get caught up in a bunch of drama before this is all over with."

"Honey, people are being healed all over the world. Surely you can't think that's wrong."

"I guess it's their faith that heals them. I'm pretty sure it's not the bottled water from Costco."

Eli pushed away from the desk and walked around to where Lenni stood. "Honey, I need you to stand down. Abraham's methods may not be to our liking, but you can't deny that people's finances are being restored; some are being healed… yes, faith is a huge part of it. Hope is a factor. I don't see anything wrong with this. We need money in order to help keep this ministry going and to be able to help all of the families we've been able to help. I focus on the results—not the method."

"Maybe it's because I see the way these same people are categorized when they're entered into the computer. They're sorted by their conditions whether it be debt or cancer. You don't think that's a bit strange?"

"Maybe it's just a way to track their testimonies. It also gives us insight as to what to pray over."

"I suppose," Lenni said. "I also think it's odd that Sophia didn't join Abraham in Maryland over the weekend and she wasn't at church yesterday."

"Maybe she visited another congregation," Eli said. "Hon, what's going on with you? Why are you suddenly so suspicious?"

"Eli, you know that I've never trusted Abraham and Sophia. I still don't, if you want to know the truth, but people are being healed. The testimonies are real. I can't refute that."

"It is people's faith in the Lord—not that packet of water. Sure, it may activate their faith, but it is that mustard seed faithing that is bringing about these testimonies."

Lenni agreed. "You're absolutely right."

"Right about what?" Sophia asked. She held up a book. "I came in to drop this off to Eli."

"We were just discussing how it's faith in God that is bringing about all the healing, and other miracles taken place in our ministry, and how it's not your husband doing this."

"Abraham has never proclaimed that he was capable of any of those things. He is just a messenger of the Lord, just like Eli."

Chapter Twenty

Phoenix touched base with her father after her first week on the job. "Dad, I'm astonished at how much money that comes in—we're talking thousands daily. The thing that bothers me is I'm sure some of these people are sending in their last dollar."

"Why do you think that?"

"I heard that most of the people reaching out are in need of financial help. They give seed money in hopes of receiving a greater financial blessing. I think it's just wrong."

"I saw his commercial the other night. One guy testified that after he drank the Anointed Water, he received a check for $4000 seven days later. There were a couple more testimonies like that. Another woman said she was healed of cancer."

"I logged $346,000 dollars today," Phoenix said. "I heard from one of my coworkers that Holy Cross took over a million dollars last week."

"Are you in the office alone?"

"No. I work with four other staff members, but I'm the only one allowed to actually handle the money. There's always a member of the security team present and I'm pretty sure we're monitored by cameras."

"What do you think they're doing with all of that money?"

"I have no idea," Phoenix murmured. "Abraham and his wife have very nice offices with expensive furnishings. I heard they live in a multi-million-dollar home. Sophia drives Maserati—well… let me clear that up. She is driven around. Shadow is her personal bodyguard and driver."

"Shadow?"

"He's the head of security. He was Abraham's bodyguard in Dallas, too."

Phoenix checked the clock. "Dad, I'll give you a call later in the week. I'm going to dinner with a friend. He should be here shortly."

"He?"

She chuckled. "*He* is just a friend, Dad. Julian lives next door."

He arrived a few minutes later.

They decided to walk to the restaurant which was located a block away.

They were seated immediately and made small talk while they waited for their food to arrive.

"New Orleans is one of my favorite places to visit," Julian was saying.

"I love it there."

"So, what made you move to North Carolina?"

"I was engaged and then we decided to call it off," Phoenix stated. "I needed fresh start."

"I'm sorry."

"It's okay. How about you? Are you a native North Carolinian?"

"I am," Julian responded with a smile. "I moved away for

about five years, but I came back when my uncle got sick. He raised me."

The waitress arrived with their food.

Julian said the blessing.

"This pizza is delicious." Phoenix wiped her mouth with her napkin. "Thank you for bringing me here."

"This is one of my favorite places to eat," Julian said. "Pizza is my guilty pleasure."

She smiled. "Mine, too."

"I'm curious," Julian said. "How do you like working for Abraham McCormick?"

Phoenix shrugged in nonchalance. "It's a job." She glanced up at him. "Have you met him?"

Julian nodded. "I have."

"What do you think of him?"

"He's charismatic and he believes in what he's doing."

Phoenix took a sip of her lemonade. "I take it that you don't."

"I focus on what the Lord has given *me* to do," Julian responded. "My church is not as large or lavish as McCormick's but I'm content. My focus is teaching my congregation the Word of God."

"You're a minister?"

He nodded. "I am."

"Oh wow… I had no idea."

Julian laughed. "You okay?"

"I'm just surprised, that's all. You don't seem like any pastor I've ever met."

"Is that a good thing?"

Phoenix smiled. "Definitely. I haven't met many pastors who seem focused on the Word, just on promising people that if they send in all of their life savings—the Lord will bless them for their faithfulness."

"By your statement, I take it that you don't believe in someone who promotes the idea that the more faith you have—the more God will bless you, love you or give you the desires of your heart."

"I guess I should clarify that I believe one should have faith. I just feel with prosperity preachers—it's more about giving to get. The whole sowing seeds in faith in order to receive something. I just don't believe that's part of the Bible," Phoenix stated. "I should also add that I don't really read mine. Therefore, I may not have a clue about anything."

Julian burst into laughter, prompting her to join in.

"What are your thoughts on this?" Phoenix inquired.

"The people that come to my church from other churches come because they're usually hurting. They are battling illness, problems in their marriage, or a loss of income. At their old church, the usual response was that the reason they weren't receiving God's favor was because they weren't believing enough." Julian wiped his mouth. "Now having said that, meeting physical needs is simply a part of ministering to the whole person."

"But Jesus is presented as the ticket to perfect heath and financial wealth," Phoenix said. "I may not read my Bible every day, but I've read enough to know that the New Testament focuses more on eternal rewards."

Julian smiled. "You do know a lil' something."

"I'm not a total heathen, huh?"

They laughed.

An hour later, Julian made sure she was in her house before he headed next door to his own.

She showered and prepared for bed, thoughts of Julian at

the forefront of her mind. Phoenix had enjoyed their conversation. She also liked the fact that he hadn't tried to cross any boundaries. There were no red flags where he was concerned, but she wasn't ready to completely let down her guard.

———

LENNI RAPPED SOFTLY on the door, causing Phoenix to look up from her computer screen. "Come in, Mrs. Carpenter."

"Just call me Lenni."

"What can I do for you?" Phoenix had seen her around from time to time in the afternoon. She had observed Lenni's interactions with Sophia enough to know that the two women couldn't stand each other.

"I just wanted to see how you're liking the job. We don't have a formal HR department, so I usually check in on our new employees."

"I have no complaints. I enjoy what I'm doing."

"Phoenix, where are you from?" Lenni asked.

"New Orleans."

"Oh," she responded. "I wouldn't have placed your accent there—I was thinking more like Oklahoma, Texas or Arizona." Lenni peered out of the window, then said, "I noticed we haven't seen you in church. Do you attend one of the other churches in the area?"

Phoenix shook her head. "No, I've been focused on getting settled in my home. I can't function until I have everything in its place. By the time I leave here during the week, I'm exhausted."

Lenni smiled. "I can relate to that. However, as an employee here, you're expected to attend at least one of the services. It's in your employment contract."

Great, Phoenix thought silently. The last thing she wanted was to spend her Sundays listening to Abraham manipulate the members of his congregation. She forced a smile. "I'll be there this coming Sunday."

"Oh, there you are," Sophia said from the doorway. "Lenni, I need you to pick up some lunch for me and Abraham. I've already ordered the food. I would go myself, but I have a meeting."

"What about Olympia?"

"She's busy," Sophia stated. "I need you to go."

Phoenix glimpsed a fleeting look of frustration that overshadowed Lenni's gaze. She could feel the heavy air of tension floating around the room.

"It was nice talking to you, Phoenix," Lenni said before storming past Sophia.

"Looks like you've made yourself at home."

She met Sophia's gaze. "Is that a problem, Mrs. McCormick?"

"No, I'm happy to see this. We pride ourselves on our family centered environment. When our employees are happy —they are more motivated to do their best work." Sophia strolled around the office. "I don't recall seeing you in service on Sunday."

Phoenix rolled her eyes heavenward. "That's because I wasn't there."

Sophia opened her mouth to speak.

"I'll be there this week," she interjected. "I wanted to get settled in my place as quickly as possible. Phoenix hoped this would put an end to the discussion of her attending church.

"Wonderful."

Phoenix rose to her feet. "I'm on my way out. I have to meet someone for lunch."

She could feel Sophia's gaze boring into her back as she made her way to her office.

Phoenix couldn't help but wonder if the woman suspected anything. She made a mental note to stay guarded whenever Sophia was around. Phoenix couldn't risk blowing her cover.

"LENNI, ARE YOU OKAY?" Phoenix asked when she encountered her in the hallway later in the day.

She nodded. "I'm fine."

"You sure?"

"Actually, I'm mad as all get out," Lenni uttered. "If I wasn't a woman of God, I'd slap Sophia McCormick so hard... that woman irritates me to no end. She calls me and Olympia her ladies-in-waiting. What kind of foolishness is that?"

Phoenix burst into laughter.

"I'm sorry. I really shouldn't have said anything."

"It's how you really feel, Lenni. It's okay. And don't worry, what you tell me stays with *me*. If you want to know the truth... I don't care for Sophia at all."

Lowering her voice to a whisper, Lenni said, "You're a smart girl, so be careful. Phoenix, she will try to get to know you—she wants to know your secrets just so that she can use them against you. Be careful around Sophia."

"I'm just the accountant... an employee."

Lenni shook her head. "She's got her eyes on you. Sophia thinks that every woman here has their eyes on Abraham, but where you're concerned—she is worried that her husband is attracted to you."

"He's been very respectful around me," Phoenix stated. "She's wrong."

"He's cheated on her," Lenni said, careful to keep her voice low. "I've seen him a couple of times with other women. I never told her. After getting to know her, I can imagine how living with a woman like Sophia would make any man stray."

Phoenix chuckled. "She is definitely something else."

Lenni placed a hand on her arm. "I'm so glad you're here. I don't have anyone to vent to when it comes to that woman. Olympia kisses Sophia's behind and I'm not doing that."

"Lenni, you can talk to me anytime," Phoenix told her.

"Thank you."

Phoenix ran into Abraham at the end of the day. She had just walked out of her office when he was locking his door.

"How are things going?" he asked her.

"Great."

"If there are some supplies you need—just write it down and give it to my secretary. We ordered two new currency counters. I appreciate you bringing it to our attention that the one we have isn't accurate."

"I count the money by hand and then reconcile it with the machine. If you ever need help, call Lenni or Olympia. They usually come by in the afternoon."

"I will," Phoenix said. "Thanks."

He walked out the building with her.

"Have you gotten settled in?" Abraham inquired.

"Pretty much," she responded. "I've already told your wife that I'll be in church on Sunday."

He laughed. "Phoenix do not let my wife bully you into coming to church. You are free to worship wherever you desire. Of course, we'd like it to be with us, but I would rather you come because it's your choice."

"It's my decision to attend on Sunday."

"Great."

"Pastor McCormick, there was a replay of one service where you told a woman to throw away her cane. How is she doing?"

"Annie Mae Riley. She's doing well."

"So, she doesn't have to use that cane at all?"

"No. She walks with a slight limp but that's about it. The Lord is good. Her daughter is in our new members class right now. She wants to help with the youth ministry. Felicia thinks that maybe she can help them stay on the right path—she doesn't want them going through some of the things she endured by being out there in the world."

"That's amazing," Phoenix said.

"In the world we live in," Abraham began, "we need to hear these types of testimonies. We need to be a light that shines in a dim environment."

"One last question, Pastor. What about the people whose lives haven't changed? Do you ever talk about them? Do you hear from them?"

"Oh yeah. I get hate mail from time to time," he admitted. "I can't guarantee miracles. I will tell anyone that this is not a quick fix. There are times when people have no faith or even a belief in God. They think of this as magic, but it's not. If you're double-minded, then you probably won't see results."

"So, do you believe that people need something tangible like Anointed Water to help them stay hopeful?"

"Possibly," Abraham responded. "Very early in my walk, I did. I had pneumonia when I was fifteen. Some of the women in my father's church made me a quilt—they prayed over it and anointed it with frankincense and myrrh." He sat his attaché case inside his car. "They covered me in that quilt, and I was healed. My lungs were clear… even the doctor said I was a miracle. Whenever I felt bad or was scared, I covered up in that quilt and prayed to God. I always felt Him near when I had it."

"Do you still have your quilt?" Phoenix wanted to know.

"Actually, I do."

"I've enjoyed this conversation, Pastor. You've given me much to think about."

"Same here, Phoenix. Enjoy your evening."

⸻

"HEY YOU…"

Phoenix glanced over her shoulder. "Julian, hello." She found herself looking forward to seeing his handsome face every day.

"I was just about to grab something to eat. Would you like to join me?"

"I'm actually making spaghetti for dinner. Why don't you come over in an hour?" she suggested. "A home cooked meal would probably do you good."

"I love spaghetti. I'll be there."

"See you then."

Julian was at her door approximately one hour later.

Phoenix bit back her smile when she let him inside. "You're just in time."

He handed her a bouquet of yellow roses.

"They're beautiful," she murmured. "I need to put them in some water."

They sat down to dinner a short time later.

She said the blessing and waited for Julian to sample his food.

He stuck a forkful in his mouth, chewed slowly, then swallowed. "I hope you made enough for me to take a plate home. This is delicious."

"There's more than enough," Phoenix said. "If you like, I'll give you a few easy recipes."

"I'd really appreciate that. I spend a lot of money eating out."

"I'm surprised you don't have some of the women at your church trying to cook for you."

He chuckled. "They would if I'd let them. I don't want any confusion regarding my intentions, so I tend to keep a professional distance. It's not easy when you're a single man in the pulpit. Speaking of which, I'd like for you to visit my church."

"I'll do that," Phoenix responded, "but first I have to attend Holy Cross. It's in my employment contract."

"You haven't attended services there? I just assumed…"

"I've been more focused on getting settled. But the truth is that I don't know if I can sit through one of Abraham's sermons. I'd rather come to your church."

"Go with an open mind, Phoenix. Hopefully, you'll be able to glean a nugget or two from the message."

"At least he has a good gospel choir," she said. "I know I'll enjoy the music if nothing else."

Julian laughed.

⬚

"GOOD MORNING," Lenni greeted on Sunday when Phoenix entered through the double doors. "I'm so glad you're here."

"Me, too," she lied. This was the last place she wanted to be and hoped Abraham wasn't long-winded.

"Eli will be bringing the message this morning."

Phoenix relaxed visibly, prompting a chuckle from Lenni. "I have to confess I have that same reaction."

"I guess I'd better find a seat."

"Come sit beside me," Lenni urged.

She felt the hair on the back of her neck stand up. Her eyes traveled the sanctuary until they landed on Sophia who was staring in her direction.

Phoenix smiled and gave a slight nod.

Sophia turned her attention back to the choir.

Clapping, Phoenix tapped her foot to the music. She could hardly wait for this service to come to an end.

Abraham and Eli entered the sanctuary and walked into the pulpit. They both knelt down almost simultaneously in front of their chairs to pray.

They sat down. Abraham's gaze bounced around the church. When he saw her, he broke into a smile.

"What was that about?" Lenni asked in a whisper.

"I think he's just surprised to see me."

"Before you even get the question out of your mouth, there is absolutely nothing going on between me and Abraham," Phoenix stated when service was over. She could tell Lenni was chomping at the bit for more information all throughout Eli's sermon.

Lenni chuckled. "I can't even lie. My mind was about to go there."

"He and I had a conversation the other day about my choice to attend any church I want. Abraham wanted to make sure I wasn't being bullied by his wife."

"I can see that. Sophia's definitely a bully."

"She can only get away with it if she's allowed to do so, Lenni."

"I only put up with her because of my husband. He works closely with Abraham and I don't want any tension between them."

Phoenix had a feeling that Lenni wasn't telling her everything, but it didn't bother her. After all, she had her own secrets.

Chapter Twenty-One

Monday morning, Phoenix went back through the payroll a second time. The name Fallon Sutherland stood out to her. She was listed under the accounting department, but they had never met.

"Knock knock…" Lenni said. "You busy?"

"Hey, I have a question for you."

"What's wrong?"

"I'm not sure," Phoenix responded. "I have a Fallon Southerland on the payroll, and she's listed in this department. I've never met her. Do you know if she's working in the warehouse? I know she doesn't work in the bookstore."

"You have time to take a quick break?"

"Sure."

Once they were outside, Lenni said, "Let's go to the park. I don't want anyone to hear us."

"What's with all the secrecy?"

As soon as they sat down at one of the picnic tables, Lenni said, "Phoenix, you replaced Fallon."

"So, you're telling me that she no longer works at Holy Cross?"

"Sophia forced Abraham to fire her because she thought the woman was sleeping with him. If Fallon's still on the payroll, I guess she was right to be worried."

"Wow…"

"Or it could be that Fallon's blackmailing Abraham," Lenni said. "I heard that right before she got fired—she was upset with him about something. Some of the staff said that he would try to talk to her, and she'd just walk away or get up and leave whenever he entered a room."

"That's interesting," Phoenix murmured.

"I don't think Sophia knows that Fallon's still getting paid —she'd have a fit. That woman loves money more than she loves Abraham."

"Should I say something?" Phoenix asked.

"I wouldn't. Not right now anyway. Besides, we know it's no secret to Abraham."

"Do you know Fallon?"

"She was only here a short time, but she was nice."

"I'd love to meet with her. I'd like to know why she's getting a paycheck from a place she no longer works."

"You sound like a detective."

Phoenix chuckled. "I'm just naturally curious."

"Well, just a word of advice to you. Don't go sticking your nose into Abraham's business. His guard dogs, especially Shadow won't like it."

"Does your husband know how unhappy you truly are with this alliance?"

"He does, but Eli feels we are exactly where we're supposed to be. He keeps telling me that God hasn't released us to leave Holy Cross."

"He could be right."

Lenni nodded. "I just don't know how much longer I can put up with that woman."

"LET'S GO AWAY SOMEWHERE," Fallon pleaded. "Just for a weekend. We could go to Myrtle Beach or even Wilmington Beach for a day. I just want to have some fun with you."

"You know I can't do that," Abraham said.

"You don't have to preach every Sunday."

"How would I explain this to my wife? Sophia, I'm taking my girlfriend on a romantic getaway. I wouldn't make it out of the house alive. Then there's the chance of being recognized. I've already had enough drama like that. I really don't want to go through it again."

"She already knows we're sleeping together," Fallon argued. "Why would it matter?"

"Trust me, it would matter to Sophia."

"You sound like you're afraid of her."

"Fallon, that's not it at all. I love my wife and I refuse to just hurt her like that. I was married before and I cheated on her with Sophia. The pain I caused my first wife—it still haunts me. She was a good woman and she loved me at a time when I didn't love myself. I took her for granted... the life I had with her... everything." Abraham shook his head in dismay. "It wasn't right. The thing is that I underestimated the depth of her devastation."

"If you feel so guilty, why do you cheat on Sophia?"

"Because it's how we started. She doesn't care if I'm unfaithful. She told me once that she expected it. However, she won't tolerate being humiliated."

"The more I get to know you, Abraham—you're really a good man. You have a heart for people, and you care."

"Don't put me on a pedestal, Fallon. You'll only be disappointed. I am a perfectly flawed individual."

"Do you enjoy being up in the pulpit?"

"It's my calling," Abraham responded. "I know that you think I'm a hypocrite, but my actions have nothing to do with my love for the Lord. I *want* to be more like Christ. It's just my flesh is weak."

"I can tell you're feeling conflicted."

"I've always let my desires take control of the decisions I've made, even as a child."

"That's normal when it comes to being children, don't you think?"

Abraham shook his head. "Not in my case. Not when the choices you make lead to someone dying."

⸺

"I THINK you should run a background check on Phoenix D'Angelo."

"What exactly is your problem with her?" Shadow inquired. "I can tell that you don't like the woman."

"I can't put my finger on it, but something's not right about her," Sophia responded. "Her references checked out. However, I can't help but feel that she's hiding something. She goes out of her way to blend in with the woodwork. It's like she wants to be invisible. I don't trust people like that."

"Maybe she just doesn't like being the center of attention." He eyed her. "Are you worried that she's caught Abraham's eye?"

"Shadow, I'm not jealous of that woman, if that's what

you're trying to say. I just prefer knowing everything about the people who work for me."

"Is it worth it?"

Sophie looked over at Shadow. "Is what worth it?"

"Putting up with Abraham's cheating."

"As long as he is discreet—I can deal with his infidelities because I focus on the bigger picture and all that we can accomplish together."

"Along with the fact that you love him."

"Yes. I love Abraham very much as you well know." She got up and walked around her desk. "Shadow don't go letting your emotions get involved with our sleeping together. It's just sex. Nothing more."

Chapter Twenty-Two

Phoenix was about to knock on Abraham's door which was slightly ajar when she heard him say Fallon's name. She couldn't hear most of what he was saying because his tone drifted in and out as if he were trying to keep his voice low.

"I can't wait to see you, too."

Her mouth dropped open as she eased back down the hall to her office. From the little she heard, Phoenix was convinced that Fallon and Abraham were lovers which debunked her blackmailing theory.

So far, all she had on Abraham was that he was having an affair. Phoenix didn't care about his marriage to Sophia. She had hoped to prove that he'd violated yet another victim. Maybe he'd been scared straight by this experience with Nadine and the other women.

Phoenix consoled herself with the fact that she might still be able to expose his fraudulent activity with the Anointed Water scam. Lenni had mentioned several angry letters from viewers who felt they'd been ripped off. Phoenix had to find a way to get copies.

"What are you thinking about?"

Olympia's voice brought Phoenix out of her reverie. "I'm sorry. Did you need something?"

"I wanted to see if you had any extra folders. I don't like keeping these letters in this box. I think we should file them away."

Her phone buzzed. Olympia grimaced.

"Everything okay?" Phoenix inquired.

"First Lady needs me. I need to head over there right now." She sat the box on the desk. "Can I leave this here? I should be back in about an hour."

"Sure. If you want, I can put them in a folder and have everything waiting for your return."

"Thank you, Phoenix."

"That was easy," she murmured to herself. *I just need to figure out a way to make copies without being seen,* she thought.

Phoenix called Lenni from her cell. "Hey, you have a minute?"

"Sure, I'm in Eli's office."

She stood up and headed down the hall.

"Where's your hubby?" Phoenix inquired.

"He and Otis are in a meeting with Abraham. What's going on?"

"Olympia just came in with a box of letters. She was looking for a folder, but then she was called away by Sophia."

"You said a box? A green one?"

Phoenix nodded. "Do you know what letters she's talking about?"

"Yes, those are the letters of people who wrote to tell us

that they have been healed of cancer or HIV. Powerful testimonies."

"Oh…" She sat down in the empty chair beside Lenni. "I thought they were the ones you told me about."

"Sophia wants us to destroy those. She's not going to keep stuff like that around—it might get in the wrong hands." Lenni glanced over her shoulder toward the door before continuing. "However, I scanned and kept copies of all of them."

"You did?"

"Yes. I can forward the file to you," Lenni said. "You never know if and when we might need that information."

"You're right about that."

"You can never let anyone know you have those files, Phoenix."

"Lenni, you can trust me."

"I know or I wouldn't have mentioned any of this to you. I hope you know that you can trust me as well."

"I'm glad to hear it."

Lenni picked up her phone. "What's your email address?"

Phoenix gave it to her.

"There's something I'd like to know… why are you really here? I don't think you just happened upon Holy Cross by chance."

Phoenix wasn't sure how to respond to Lenni's question. "Why do you say that?"

"You're deliberate in your actions. I see the way you observe everything that's going on around you. It's like you're taking notes in your head or something."

"You have an overactive imagination," Phoenix said with a chuckle. "But the truth is that I don't buy completely into Abraham McCormick. I believe about 50% of what comes out of his mouth. He may seem genuine but as far as I'm concerned—he's nothing but a scammer."

"That's it," Lenni said. "You think he scammed someone you know and you're trying to prove it. That's why you want these letters, right?"

"Something like that."

"Are you a reporter?"

"No, I'm not," Phoenix managed. "I just hate when people like Abraham and Sophia take advantage of people who work hard for their money. I know they only ask for $20 but people send in hundreds and some thousands of dollars, hoping to buy a miracle. I'm still in shock over people charging their tithes to a credit card—they're creating debt. I can't even tell you how many checks are returned because Abraham tells people to trust God for the payment. When they bounce, we charge fees and threaten them with fraudulent check charges if they don't pay. It makes me sick."

Lenni nodded in agreement. "I'm sure you know that Abraham's been under fire before."

"You're talking about the rape charges?"

She nodded a second time. "The man I've gotten to know doesn't seem capable of doing what those women said... Pastor Connor—he was the one who bought Abraham to Holy Cross. He was once accused of rape. He was proven innocent."

"And he believes the same of Abraham," Phoenix said.

"Yes."

"Lenni, all I can say is that one day his luck is going to run out. He will have to face the consequences of his actions." Phoenix rose to her feet. "I'd better get back to work."

SHE AND LENNI decided to have lunch in the park area of the church away from the eyes and ears of the other employees.

"I'm so frustrated," Lenni complained. "Sophia is getting on my last nerve. She walks around treating me and Olympia like her servants. Every time I try to talk to Eli about this—he just keeps saying that God hasn't put it on his heart to leave."

"I take it you don't share that same belief."

"I hate being around Sophia. She's self-centered and manipulative. I just can't stand her, but my hands are tied. As long as Eli is here—I will remain by his side." She bit into her sandwich, chewing slowly.

"I don't care for some of the stuff that goes on in some church settings, Lenni. Like here at Holy Cross."

"I agree with you there. Sophia's had a whole new database set up and she's hired fifteen people for that department to enter donor information into the system," Lenni bit into her sandwich, chewing slowly. "Girl, they are putting it under things like in debt, got cancer or some other terminal illness. She then has them shredding the evidence so it can't be traced back to Abraham. He never sees any of the letters."

"Really?"

Lenni nodded. "I think he's primarily concerned with how much money comes in. The board just agrees to everything Abraham wants and Sophia..." she stopped short. "She will do whatever she has to do to get what she wants."

Phoenix studied Lenni. "She has something on you, doesn't she?"

"Sophia discovered something about me that Eli doesn't know, and he can never find out, so basically I'm at her mercy. I hate being in this position."

"Have you tried looking into her closet of secrets?" Phoenix suggested.

"I know why they left Dallas, but that's about it." After a moment, Lenni said, "Sophia know about my relationship with another woman. It's been over a while, but…"

"You don't have to talk about it if you're uncomfortable."

"Elizabeth and I were roommates in college. One night after I broke up with this guy I was seeing at the time, I was so heartbroken. Things… things just happened. I love Eli, Phoenix, but it was something about her."

"You don't have to explain yourself, Lenni."

"He can't ever find out. Eli takes a hard stance on same sex relationships. I believe he'd divorce me."

"Maybe not," Phoenix said. "He loves you just as much as you love him. I see it every time he looks at you."

"I'm so ashamed."

Phoenix handed her a tissue. "How did Sophia find out?"

"She must have had Shadow or some detective following me," Lenni stated. "She has pictures of Elizabeth and I together."

"Compromising photographs?"

"Yes."

"Oh wow, she really is something else." Phoenix finished off her salad. "We have to pay her back in kind."

"What do you mean?"

"It's time we started searching through her closet. Let's see what comes out when we open that door."

━━━

"THAT MUST BE QUITE some conversation between those

two," Sophia said, watching Lennies and Phoenix from her office window. "I wonder what or who they're discussing."

"When did you start caring about office gossip?"

"Shadow, I don't trust either of them."

Sophia was not thrilled with Lenni's burgeoning friendship with Phoenix D'Angelo. "I'm going to have to keep my eye on those two."

"You don't have anything to worry about."

"How can you be so sure?"

"Lenni's too afraid to cross you. As for Phoenix... she seems more interested in getting to know her next door neighbor, Julian Nelson."

"Pastor Julian Nelson?" Sophia inquired.

Shadow gave a slight nod. "The two of them spend quite a bit of time together."

"He's a handsome man. It's a shame he pastors such a tiny church."

"Not everyone wants a megachurch, Sophia."

She glanced over at Shadow and whispered, "You don't know how bad I want to leave right now. I'm just not in the mood to deal with these employees today."

"What's wrong with you? I've never seen you act like this."

"I don't know, Shadow. I just have this feeling of dread. My stomach is in knots. I feel anxious."

"C'mon, I'll take you home."

Sophia looked as if she was about to break down in sobs at any given moment. "I don't know what's going on with me."

"Maybe you're just tired," Shadow offered. "You'll go home. I'll make you some tea. You try to relax and get some rest."

Chapter Twenty-Three

Julian invited Phoenix to attend a scholarship banquet that was held at his church.

She felt at home in the quaint little building which was the size of one of the banquet halls at Holy Cross. "I love the intimate setting," she told Julian.

"I grew up in this church. My uncle and my grandfather pastored here. I always knew that I'd come back home and do the same."

"This is your legacy," she responded.

His was peering intently at her.

"What? Do I have something on my face?"

"No, you're just so beautiful, Phoenix. I love spending time with you."

"I feel the same way about you."

After the choir sang, it was time for Julian to give his keynote address.

He was eloquent, but not showy or charismatic like Abraham. Julian's delivery of his message was genuine and came from the heart.

Their friendship was evolving into something more. Phoenix could feel it and she knew Julian felt it too.

As their evening drew to a close and they were back at her place, he confirmed her thoughts when he said, "I want to take our friendship to the next level. I care a great deal for you, Phoenix."

She took his hand in hers. "I feel the same way."

He kissed her.

After her break-up with Dylan, she wasn't sure she'd ever be able to love another person, but Phoenix was wrong. She was falling hard for Julian, a pastor.

Amused by the irony, she smiled.

"What are you thinking about?" Julian asked.

"I came here with the belief that all people who claimed to be called to minister were full of crap," Phoenix stated. "My belief was based on all the negativity I've heard about priests, nuns, pastors, bishops—every title you can imagine. I didn't grow up in church, so I don't really have a point of reference to indicate otherwise." She planted a kiss on Julian's lips. "Until tonight."

Her eyes filled with tears. "Everything you talked about in your keynote was scriptural. You never made it about money and it was a scholarship banquet. You made it about God. The nuggets you gave those students… I can apply to my own life, Julian." She wiped her eyes. "I didn't mean to get emotional but I've never felt this way before. Thank you for giving me a different perspective. You've given me hope that there are more men like you in pulpits."

"There are," Julian said. "Both my grandfather and my uncle were men of great faith. My father wasn't in the pulpit

—he was a minister of music. He died when I was eight. My uncle and aunt raised me. I have always been surrounded by men who seek after God. It's all I know."

He was so handsome, so genuine… guilt snaked down her spine. She was not being completely honest with him and while Phoenix wanted nothing more than to tell him everything—she couldn't.

ABRAHAM SAT at the head of the conference table fighting boredom. He hated the monthly budget meetings. When his phone buzzed for the seventh or eighth time within the last hour, he checked his watch, then said, "Let's take a ten-minute break."

"Fallon, why have you been texting me all day?" Abraham demanded when he entered his office, closing the door behind him. "I told you I'd be in a meeting this evening."

"This is important, Abraham. I really need to talk to you," she responded. "You know I haven't been feeling well."

"Did you see a doctor?" he asked. "I heard there was some kind of virus going around."

"Yeah, I went this morning."

Distracted, Abraham scrolled through his emails. "So, are you okay?" He wasn't in the mood for another one of her tantrums.

"We need to talk," Fallon insisted. "Face to face."

"Why?"

"Abraham, I don't want to do this over the phone. I need to see you right away."

He sighed in frustration. "Fallon, I don't have time for this. I have to get back to my meeting."

"I'm pregnant," she blurted. "I didn't want to tell you this way."

He was stunned into silence.

When he found his voice, he uttered, "I'll be there as soon as I'm done here."

"I'll see you then, Abraham."

Forty-five minutes later, he was letting himself into her apartment with his key.

Fallon was waiting for Abraham in the bedroom dressed in a sexy pink and blue teddy.

"Can you believe it?" she asked. "We're having a baby."

He shook his head in denial. "Naaaw... there's no way."

Her smile vanished. "I disagree. You're the only man I've been with. This child I'm carrying is yours. I'm more than happy to take a DNA test."

"Fallon, listen to me. My wife and I have tried for years and it's just not possible. You can't be pregnant by me."

"Maybe it was Sophia who had the problem."

"You can't have this child."

"I'm not having an *abortion*, Abraham."

"Do you have any idea what this will do to my marriage? Sophia not only leave me. She'll also take everything I've worked so hard for—I won't let that happen." He paced the length of the hardwood floor. "I'm so close to having enough money to renovate that old apartment building—the one where I grew up."

"I didn't get pregnant on purpose, Abraham. We used protection and it failed. This child is meant to be. Don't you see that? It's a blessing and you're trying to treat it as a curse."

"All I see is the end of everything."

"I'm giving you the child that Sophia can't," Fallon said.

"You told me once that you wanted a son. That you didn't want your bloodline to end."

"I didn't want to have a child with you."

Fallon drew back as if she'd been slapped. "Get out."

"I didn't mean it the way it sounded," Abraham stated. "I wanted a child with my wife. Look, this is a lot to deal with right now."

"I'm gonna have my baby with or without you. I only told you because I owe you that much, but what I won't do is stand here and allow you to disrespect me. I didn't get pregnant by myself. You knew you were chasing after me."

"Don't try to rewrite history, Fallon. You were always in my face flirting and throwing your ample breasts in my face. I'm a man. What did you expect me to do?"

"You dipped in my pool and now you've caught yourself a baby. We're both in this situation and fighting is not gonna solve a thing."

"You're right," Abraham said. "Fallon, I apologize. I know this isn't your fault."

"It's not like we planned this," she responded.

"There's no doubt that you're pregnant?"

"If there was, I never would've said anything until I knew for sure. Abraham, I don't play games like that. This came as a complete surprise to me. Do you want me to take a DNA test?"

Abraham shook his head. "I believe you. I have to warn you that this is going to get really ugly if Sophia finds out."

"I don't care about your wife or your money. The thing important to me right now is this child that I'm carrying."

"I need some time to process this news. I hope you understand."

"I do," Fallon responded. "Take all the time you need. This baby isn't going anywhere."

———

FALLON WATCHED ABRAHAM DRIVE AWAY, then made a phone call.

"How did it go?"

"He's in total shock," she responded. "I almost feel bad for him."

"Don't. He's a serial rapist dressed in designer suits. Trust me, he's not the man you think he is."

"I have a feeling that he's going to want proof that I'm pregnant."

"Well, give it to him. You *are* pregnant, right?"

Placing a hand to her belly, she smiled. "Yeah, I am."

"This is the beginning of the end for Abraham McCormick."

"You really think he's going to lose everything for this baby?" Fallon asked. "I know the one thing he wants most is a child, but I don't think he will willingly walk away from Sophia."

"He won't have to—she'll leave him."

———

ABRAHAM'S MIND was all over the place.

A *baby*… Sophia would be devastated by the news, but not only that—she would divorce him and take every single penny in their bank account.

When he arrived home, Abraham went straight to his office. He figured Sophia would be upstairs asleep. After

Fallon's announcement about the baby, he was wide awake and didn't want to risk disturbing her.

"You look really worried about something," Sophia stated when she entered his office. She settled down on the small loveseat. "Why don't you just tell me what's wrong?"

"I'm just thinking about everything that needs to be done before the month is out."

"Did you get a chance to read over the revised donor letter I emailed to you?" she asked. "We need to send them out as soon as possible."

"What's wrong with the one Eli wrote?"

Sophia sat down in one of the visitor's chairs facing his desk. "It's good to switch them up, Abraham. They're supposed to be *personalized* letters from you. I had someone create a font that closely matches your handwriting. This particular letter tells our potential donors that God has been speaking to you about their problems and you want to help."

"But it gives the impression that I'll only help them if they send money to the ministry."

"This type letter is one used throughout the direct mail marketing world, Abraham," Sophia explained. "You tell them that the Lord has put a burden on your heart, and you couldn't sleep until…"

"Until I reached out to them."

She nodded. "Right. It doesn't mention a donation or anything—it's just about this great burden on your heart. They will send money out of gratitude."

Sophia scanned his face. "I don't like when you keep secrets, Abraham. I can read you like a book. There's always been a part of your life that you've kept locked away from me —I can accept that because that was before we got married."

"I haven't wanted to frighten you," Abraham stated. "I've

received a couple of letters with threats. That's why I had Shadow hire more security guards. That's why he's your constant companion."

"Why would you keep this from me?"

"You're shaking, sweetheart. This is why I didn't want you to know." Abraham embraced her.

"When did the last letter come?"

"A couple months ago."

"I think we should consider getting a gun," Sophia said. "We could get Shadow to teach us how to use it."

"Absolutely not," Abraham said. "I don't want a gun in my house."

Chapter Twenty-Four

Outside of Abraham's office, Phoenix debated whether or not to interrupt his conversation with Sophia.

She decided now wasn't the best time and headed to the break room. She'd give him the reports later.

Phoenix wasn't surprised that he'd been receiving hate mail. She was sure not everyone bought into his propaganda. She'd heard about the bag of dog filth which amused her greatly. It was just what he'd deserved. Phoenix was more surprised that he didn't receive more of it on a daily basis.

She was curious though. Did the letters have to do with the Anointed Water or the fact that he'd gotten away with attacking her friend and the other women? Were they delivered through the mail or had they come via email? She knew that Abraham insisted on opening any mail that came with his name affixed to it.

But why would he need to increase security?

The question lingered in her mind. He'd told Sophia that they were threatening. Phoenix surmised that they most likely had to do with the rape charges. Possibly even from the women themselves.

She thought about the night Abraham was shot. Nadine's sister called the hospital to speak to her because she wasn't answering her cell. Phoenix didn't think anything of it at the time, but now as she recalled her friend never showed up that evening.

Nadine spent a considerable amount of time at a shooting range. She told Phoenix that it made her feel powerful.

Did Nadine shoot Abraham that night? Is that why she suddenly dropped the charges?

Phoenix grabbed her phone and left the building. She sat in her car and pressed the keypad, dialing her friend's number.

"Cynthia, what is going on? I tried to call you and it keeps going to voicemail."

"I'm sorry. Look, I can't explain anything to you right now, but I'm in the middle of an investigation."

"What?"

"I promise I'll explain everything when I can. Nadine, I have to ask you something."

"Sure. What is it?"

"Did you shoot Abraham McCormick?"

"I can't believe you'd ask me something like that."

"Nadine…"

"Cynthia, call me when you're not talking crazy," she uttered before ending the conversation.

Phoenix called back but Nadine let it go to voicemail.

"That went well," she whispered. After she thought some more about it—there was no way Nadine would've gone after Abraham.

She decided to give it a couple of days before she called back to apologize.

⊏⊐

"LENNI, COME IN," Sophia said. "And close the door behind you."

"Olympia said you wanted to see me."

"Have a seat," Sophia urged.

When Lenni sat down, Sophia met her gaze. "I notice you've been spending a lot of time with Phoenix D'Angelo lately."

"We talk here at the office and have lunch together from time to time," Lenni responded.

Leaning back in her chair, Sophia asked, "What do you know about her?"

"Only that she's from Louisiana and a really nice person."

"*That's it?*" Sophia asked. "What on earth do you two discuss when you're having lunch?"

"We both love books, so we talk about what we're reading; we talk about our favorite TV shows. Just pretty general conversations."

"Does she ever talk about a boyfriend or girlfriend?"

"No, she doesn't."

"Don't you find that odd?"

"Not really. I get the feeling she wants to keep her private life private, Sophia."

"Perhaps I'm not asking the right questions. Has she ever mentioned Julian Nelson?"

"The pastor? No, she hasn't. I don't know what this is about, but I'm not going to interrogate Phoenix." Lenni knew of Phoenix's relationship with Julian but she wasn't about to tell Sophia anything.

"Hmmm... maybe I should invite her to lunch one day this week. I guess it's up to me to get to know her better.

Besides, if it's true that she and Julian are a couple... well, I need to talk to her."

"Why are you so interested?"

"Because she is handling my money."

"You mean the ministry's money, don't you?"

Sophia sent a sharp glare in Lenni's direction. "You can leave."

"Gladly."

An hour later, Sophia left her office and walked briskly toward the finance department. She stood in the doorway watching Phoenix for a moment before saying, "I'd like you to join me for lunch on Wednesday at noon."

"I'd like that," Phoenix responded, pasting on a smile. "Thank you for the invitation."

As soon as Sophia left her office, she groaned. *I don't want to sit down and share a meal with this woman. Please let this be over soon.*

━━━

"I HEARD about your lunch date with *Lady* Sophia," Lenni said when she caught up with Phoenix in the parking lot. "I hope you know what you're doing. She's heard about you and Julian."

"I'm not stupid, Lenni. I know she's on a fact-finding mission," Phoenix said with a nonchalant shrug. "However, Sophia's going to be greatly disappointed. I don't have any deep dark secrets to share with her and I'm not about to share my social life with her."

"Trust me, if you do—she'll find out," Lenni cautioned. "I believe she has Shadow spying on us. He doesn't say much but I find him very intimidating. I heard that he's a former FBI agent."

Phoenix shrugged in nonchalance. "I'm not worried about him."

"Will let me give you a heads up. She is going to ask you about your personal life—like if you're dating. She might be worried that Abraham will take an interest in you."

"My private life is just that. *Private.*"

"That won't mean anything to Sophia."

Phoenix paused in her steps. "Lenni, she can ask me anything she wants—I'm not telling her squat. I've been here long enough for my work to speak for itself. This is all Sophia needs to be concerned about."

Chapter Twenty-Five

On her way to her car, Phoenix saw Abraham pacing in his office before she left the building. She knocked softly on his door.

He smiled. "Calling it a night?"

"Yes. It's almost seven-thirty." She scanned his face. "Are you okay? You look worried."

"I have some things weighing heavy on my mind right now," he confessed.

"Is there anything I can do?" Phoenix asked, pretending to be concerned. "I'm a good listener if you need to talk."

"To be honest, I would appreciate it—I won't take up too much of your time."

Phoenix sat down.

Abraham left the door open, putting her somewhat at ease.

"I've always been comfortable with my flaws, but right now, I really wish I was a better man. I've done some things I don't ever think I can come back from."

"If I came to you feeling this way, what would you tell me, Pastor McCormick?"

He gave her one of his compelling smiles. "I would probably say that although you may go back along a trail you've been traveling—the one thing you don't want in your Christian walk is to go backwards spiritually, but if you do… you can always turn around and head in the right direction. It's never too late."

"I suppose it's easier for you to tell others than to follow your own advice," Phoenix stated.

"If I can be transparent, I've deliberately chosen to indulge in this life's sinful pleasures which I know carries disastrous consequences. I know that it brings dishonor to the One who laid down his life for me. In my heart, I want to be a better man. I hate the turmoil and condemnation that plagues my life."

In that moment, Phoenix knew Abraham was sincere. It was no act—his vulnerability in the moment. "So, what are you going to do about it?"

"I have no choice but to accept the consequences of my actions. I strive to do better each day—I mean it."

"I'm not the one you have to convince, Pastor McCormick."

"You really are a good listener, Phoenix. Not one time did you ask me for specifics—most people would want to know all the sordid details of my life."

"I'm not that way. I value my privacy and I assume others do as well." She headed to the door. Phoenix paused long enough to say, "I do like your plan for renovating apartments for the homeless. It's admirable."

"I'll walk you to your car."

As she drove out of the parking lot, Phoenix didn't know

how to interpret what just transpired with her and Abraham. Tonight, she saw him vulnerable and maybe even a little afraid.

—

"SO, TELL ME ABOUT YOURSELF, PHOENIX," Sophia said when they met for lunch on Friday afternoon. "I'd like to get to know you better."

"There isn't much to tell," she responded. "I'm from New Orleans and I'm an only child of parents who were only children themselves."

"I'm sorry to hear that. You don't have a lot of family then?"

"I don't, but it's okay. I have some wonderful people in my life—they're my support system."

"You've been here in Raleigh for a few months now. Have you met anyone special?"

Phoenix almost laughed out loud. Sophia couldn't get more obvious than that. "I have made quite a few friends in the area," she said.

"I see."

Sophia decided to try a different approach. "Since you don't have any family here and if you ever need someone to talk to—I want you to know that I'm here for you."

"Thank you, but I'm fine."

Sophia eyed her. "You don't care for me. I can tell."

"It's not that at all," Phoenix stated. "I just prefer to keep a professional distance. I want to keep my personal and work life separate."

Sofia's mouth tightened, conveying her frustration.

Her reaction amused Phoenix, but she kept her expression neutral. "I hope I haven't offended you."

"No, of course not."

Phoenix smiled. "Wonderful to hear." Changing the subject, she said, "This salmon is grilled to perfection. It's delicious."

"I'm glad you're enjoying your meal. This is a favorite restaurant of mine." She took a sip of her iced tea. "I see you and Lenni are getting along well."

"I'd like to think that I get along with everyone," Phoenix responded.

"Of course," Sophia murmured. "It just seems that you and Lenni spent a lot of time together. It's nothing wrong with it."

"We both enjoy reading, so we get together to talk books." Phoenix bit back a smile at the frustration on Sophia's face. She wasn't going to tell Sophia anything.

Sophia finally gave up the interrogation somewhere between the appetizers and the waiter returning with their food.

They spent the rest of the time discussing Holy Cross financials. Phoenix was careful not to talk specifics regarding the payroll.

"I had mixed feelings about you when Abraham hired you, but I must admit—you're very good at your job."

"Thank you," she responded. "I'm enjoying it."

Phoenix was prepared to pay for her meal, but Sophia insisted. "This is my treat. Perhaps we'll do it again one day."

Not if I can help it, she thought to herself.

"I KNOW I'm being nosy, but I have to ask... how did your lunch with Sophia go?"

"Not exactly as she planned, I'm sure," Phoenix responded with a chuckle.

"I hope you know that you've gained an enemy," Lenni said.

Shrugging in nonchalance, Phoenix said, "I don't care. I'm not here looking to make friends with Pastor McCormick or his wife."

"You're the first person I've met who isn't afraid of Sophia."

"Are you afraid of her?" Phoenix inquired.

"Not really, but most of the people who work here—they find her very intimidating. Even Olympia."

"Have you thought any more about what we talked about?"

Lenni's eyes filled with tears. "I can't do this to Eli. Phoenix, he's a real good man. I don't want to break his heart."

"It will hurt him more if he finds out from someone other than you," Phoenix advised.

"When you feel the time is right... talk to your husband. I can tell that he really loves you, Lenni.

I believe that the two of you can get pass this."

"You really believe that?"

"I do."

"I pray so. I don't want to lose my husband," Lenni said. "I have to really think this out."

Chapter Twenty-Six

"What's wrong with you?" Abraham inquired when Sophia blew through the door of his office.

"I just took Phoenix out for a nice lunch and the twit had the audacity to tell me that she prefers to keep her personal and professional lives separate. In other words, she was basically telling me to mind my own business."

He broke into an amused grin. "I'm sure you didn't like that."

"I was making an attempt to get to know her."

"Well, clearly she's not interested."

"Why do you find this so entertaining?"

"Because you're all upset for no reason. Phoenix is entitled to a personal life—one that we have nothing to do with or should know about."

"She's dating Julian Nelson. Did you know that?"

"No, I didn't and why should I care?"

"She could be telling him how much money we got coming in here, Abraham."

He chuckled. "I don't believe she'd do something like that." Looking in her eyes, Abraham questioned, "How do you know who she's seeing?"

"I heard it through the Holy Cross grapevine. You know how people like to gossip."

"What do you have against Phoenix?"

"I feel like she's hiding something," Sophia stated. "She's very vague about everything."

"It's her personal business."

"Abraham, we don't know anything about this woman. I don't like it."

"Phoenix is good at her job. That's all I care about."

"That's how things went left the first time. Then that woman contacted Cynthia Highcloud with that lie. Before the interview ended, others had jumped onto the bandwagon. You do remember that, don't you? Not only were we humiliated… we lost everything, Abraham."

"Sophia, you have to stop living in the past. We're not doing anything wrong."

"We really didn't do anything *wrong* back then either," she countered. "You were innocent, but the public didn't care. That reporter obviously didn't care about the truth."

"Things are different now," Abraham assured her. "This time all of our bases are covered." He gently brushed a curly tendril away from Sophia's face. "You have nothing to worry about."

She was clearly not convinced.

―――

"I WAS BEGINNING to think that I'd never hear from you

again," Fallon said. "You haven't returned any of my texts or calls."

"I told you I would need some time to process everything."

"And?"

"I haven't had a change of heart, Fallon."

"I told you that I'm not having an abortion."

"I wasn't going to suggest that. I was going to say that it would be best if you leave town for a while."

"You want to send me away?"

"We can't risk my wife finding out about this child, Fallon."

"I don't care if she knows," she responded. "We made this baby together and we should raise it together."

"Look Fallon... I will pay child support but I'm not leaving Sophia."

"If I tell her about the baby—she'll leave you."

"You'd better not say a word."

"What are you gonna do about it, Abraham? Are you gonna hit me?"

"No... Fallon, why do you want to destroy me?"

"All I want is to be with you. Abraham, I love you and I thought you felt the same way about me."

"I care for you, Fallon, but..."

"But nothing," she interjected. "Abraham, don't you want to be with the woman you love? Don't you want to raise your child? You can't convince me that you want to give up your happiness because you and Sophia make a great team. I know you don't love her."

"That's where you're wrong. I *do* love my wife."

Shaking her head, Fallon responded, "I don't believe you."

WHILE ABRAHAM WAS ENTERTAINING his mistress, Sophia spent the evening in the arms of Shadow in the guesthouse. When they purchased the house, she'd convinced her husband that they needed an estate with enough room to house their security team.

"Have you found out anything on Miss Phoenix D'Angelo?"

"Not yet," he responded. "For the most part, she seems to have led a normal life with no incidents. Although I must admit it seems to be a little too perfect. Sophia, I'm telling you that you have nothing to worry about where she's concerned."

"You're probably right."

Shadow glanced at the clock on the nightstand. "It's getting late. I should walk you back to house."

Sophia shrugged. "I'm sure Abraham's with Fallon. He won't be home until late." She glanced over at Shadow. "I really don't want to be alone right now. I can't seem to shake this funk I've been in."

Shadow embraced her. "I wish there was something I could do to help you. I hate seeing you this way."

"I hate feeling like this, but I can't help myself." Sophia leaned against his chest. "Maybe I'm going through a depression or something. I've always wanted a house full of children," Sophia said. "I gave up on that dream after my sixth attempt at invitro. Abraham and I tried for ten years. It's taken an emotional toll on both of us. I've been thinking a lot about babies lately."

"I'm sorry."

"So am I. I think that's why I don't begrudge Abraham his flings. However, if a child ever comes out of one—it would kill me. I can't bear the thought of another woman giving my husband the one thing he wants most and something I couldn't give him. It's the one thing that makes me feel less than a woman."

"You're all woman and more."

Sophia smiled. "You make me feel like I'm the only woman in the world. It's a shame we didn't meet a long time ago. Maybe things would've turned out differently."

Chapter Twenty-Seven

"Phoenix, come in," Abraham said.

"Here are the reports you asked for." She placed the document on his desk.

"Thank you." He looked away from his computer monitor. "I want you to know that I really appreciate all the work you've done."

She smiled. "I'm just doing my job, Pastor McCormick."

"I also appreciate your discretion. I'm sure you are aware that there's no Fallon Sutherland on staff."

"It's really not my business."

"She once held the position that you're holding now. I let her go because Sophia demanded it."

"You don't owe me any explanations."

"The reason I'm telling you this, Phoenix is because I'm gotten myself in a situation. One that involves an unborn child."

"Oh…"

"I need to make sure she has everything she needs. I want

to increase the payments by a thousand dollars. I'm sure you can understand why I don't want to put that in writing."

The animation had left his face. "This is a real mess but it's one of my doing. I apologize for having to involve you in this. However, I give you my word—nothing will come back on you, Phoenix."

"I'll do as you requested."

Phoenix didn't feel an ounce of pity for the situation Abraham found himself in—this was going to blow up in his face and she wanted to be in the front seat. Like Gerald, he deserved this and more.

"YOU BOUGHT ME FLOWERS?"

"It's my way of apologizing for the way I've behaved, Fallon." He kissed her gently on the lips. "This just took me completely by surprise."

"I know that this is all new for you, Abraham."

"I want you to know that I genuinely care for you. But I also love my wife."

"I'm not sure you love Sophia as much as you think," Fallon stated. "She's comfortable for you. She accepts you just as you are… I get it."

"I've always wanted children. Lots of them. As many as I could afford." Abraham clasped his hands together. "Sophia and I tried everything."

"I'm carrying your child," Fallon reminded him gently.

"I know. A part of me is thrilled that I'm going to be a father, but the other part… this is going to devastate my wife."

"I can't make this decision for you, Abraham. You have to decide how you're going to handle this situation."

"What are you hoping will happen?"

"I'd like for us to raise our son or daughter together."

"I want the same. As much as I love Sophia… I can't bear the thought of not being in my child's life full-time."

"I think you know that you can't have us both. You will have to choose between Sophia and me."

"It can't be any other way," Abraham said. "I will never abandon my child."

"I'm going to put these in some water. I'll be right back."

Abraham sat staring off into space. It was true—he loved Sophia and he firmly believed that she was his soulmate. But he cared for Fallon as well.

"I'm going to have to find the right time to tell Sophia," he said when Fallon returned. "Can I trust you to keep your pregnancy quiet? This is going to break her heart."

"Although she's always treated me like crap and had me fired—I don't wish her any ill will," Fallon said.

"I CAN'T KEEP DOING this to Abraham," Fallon told her visitor. "He doesn't deserve this."

"Oh, trust me… he deserves this and more."

"What did he do to you?"

No response.

"He came by here today and we talked. He wants to be a part of the baby's life. He's choosing me. He asked me to keep quiet for now until he can find the right time to tell Sophia. He's nothing like the man you described."

Harsh laughter rang out. "You believe that lie? That man only loves himself and money."

"You're wrong. I carry his child."

More laughter. "You think that matters to him?"

"I want out. I can't keep deceiving him like this. Not if I want a future with him."

"It's too late for that. We stick to the plan."

"I can't," Fallon said. "I just want to focus on having a healthy pregnancy and spending the rest of my life with Abraham. I don't want to be a part of this anymore. I'm done."

"I hope you're not thinking of doing something stupid like telling him our little secret."

"Of course not," she responded. "I promise I won't say a word. Just let me go."

Chapter Twenty-Eight

Lenni went inside of Hammond's Men's Store to pick up the new suit she'd ordered for Eli's upcoming birthday. Near the back of the store, she heard a man talking and peeked.

It was Abraham. He was with one of the seamstresses being fitted for a black pinstripe suit. They were laughing and flirting, he didn't even notice her.

Lenni knew she was in no position to judge, but it wasn't right that Abraham was behaving so blatant with his infidelity.

She walked up to him and said, "Katrina, do you mind taking a break. I need to speak with Pastor McCormick."

Clearly, irritated, he stared back at her. "About what?"

"Abraham, have you lost your mind?" Lenni asked. "You do know that girl's parents are members of Holy Cross? Deacon White is her grandfather. I would think with all the trouble you've had in the past—you'd be more careful."

"I was only talking to the young lady," he responded. "There's no sin against that, is there?"

"I heard you. You asked her out on a date."

"I wasn't being serious."

"Abraham, a man in your position should know better."

"If I were you, I'd mind my own business."

"Mrs. Carpenter, your package is ready," the cashier announced.

Disgusted, Lenni sent him a sharp glare before walking over to the counter. She quickly paid for her purchase and left the store.

━━━

KATRINA RETURNED. "I don't know how Pastor Eli puts up with that woman. She's always got something to say about everything."

"Are you sure you can get this done by Saturday?" he asked.

"Yes," she responded with a smile.

"Don't disappoint me."

━━━

ELI LOOKED up from the computer monitor when his wife entered his office. The look on her prompted him to ask, "What's wrong, hon?"

"You wouldn't believe what I just saw," she said as she dropped down in one of the chairs facing his desk.

"I'm listening."

"Abraham was in Hammond's flirting with Deacon White's granddaughter."

Eli frowned. "Katrina?"

Lenni nodded.

"I can't believe he'd do something so careless," Eli uttered. "You'd think he'd learned from that last experience."

"I can't stay in this church with that man."

"Hon…"

Lenni shook her head. "No, Eli… if we don't leave now— He and Sophia are going to drag us down in the muck with them. She's messing around with Shadow and—"

"What?" Eli interjected. "Do you know this to be true or is this something you've heard on the Holy Cross Grapevine?"

"I've seen them together. It's the way they look at each other and how she's always touching him. Sophia's sleeping with Shadow." Lenni shifted in her seat. "And another thing you should know. Abraham has Fallon Sutherland on payroll still. I'd bet my last dime that she's his mistress."

Eli was speechless.

"This can't be the church God has for us," Lenni said. "Not with all this messiness going on. God is a God of order. You say this all the time. I know you've been waiting on a sign from the Lord releasing us from Holy Cross. I would say this is it. It's time for us to leave."

Releasing a long sigh, Eli leaned back in his chair. "You may be right."

"I'm going home to make dinner," Lenni announced. "I just can't stay here a moment longer."

"I should be there around five-thirty."

She smiled. "Don't be late. I'm making a special dinner for your birthday."

"I love you, hon."

"I love you, too, Eli."

Just as she was about to drive away, Abraham drove up and parked in his assigned space. She waited, watching him in her rearview mirror.

He smiled and waved at her as if nothing had transpired in the store earlier.

Something tugged at her memory, but Lenni couldn't grasp hold of it. It's probably nothing, she told herself.

On the drive home, Lenni prayed Eli would have a change of heart and resign his position. She didn't want to spend another Sunday under Abraham McCormick's leadership. Joel Connor had placed his faith in the wrong man. Too bad he'd passed away six months after stepped down. They found out later that he had an aggressive form of prostate cancer. He and Mary had decided to keep their battle a private one. After his death, Mary moved to Florida with her daughter.

An hour later, Lenni sat down at her computer while the roast she was making for dinner was in the oven.

She pulled up her Internet searches for Abraham, checking to see if there was anything new. On a whim, she decided to listen to the news broadcast when the rape allegations first came out.

Lenni settled back in her chair as Cynthia Highcloud discussed the charges against Abraham. Realization dawned on her. Cynthia's voice…

"It's you," she whispered. She had always known that Phoenix was hiding something. She read up on the accident and understood why she didn't look like her former self. Lenni couldn't help but wonder if Abraham was responsible.

She shook her head no. He was a whoremonger, but a killer… Lenni didn't think so, but then she didn't know for sure —after all, he'd been accused of rape. Now Shadow… he was another story.

Nobody knows his real name. Except for Abraham and Sophia… and me. Lenni had gone nosing around the employee files when she discovered his legal name was Jackson Daniels.

On impulse, she did a search.

Lenni found his military records and a couple of photos of him being awarded medals for heroic actions; it was stuff anyone could find on the internet—nothing incriminating, much to her disappointment.

She was about to give up when she saw a photograph of Shadow's unit. "Now this is pretty interesting."

Lenni couldn't wait to talk to Phoenix.

Chapter Twenty-Nine

"Eli is going to turn in his resignation tonight," Lenni announced.

"You finally got him to reconsider. I'm happy for you, but I'm going to miss your sunny smile around this building."

"I feel the same way about you." Lenni paused a moment, then said, "Phoenix, do you mind if we go for a walk?"

"Not at all. I could use a break."

When they were outside, Lenni said, "I know who you really are?"

"What are you talking about?"

"You're Cynthia Highcloud. Don't worry I don't intend to say a word to anyone about your real identity."

"How did you find out?"

"I have an ear for voices, but it was completely by accident. I ran across the interview and listened to it." Lenni glanced over her shower than back at Phoenix. "You're still investigating Abraham, aren't you?"

"I am."

"I want to help."

Phoenix shook her head no. "Lenni, you and Eli are leaving Holy Cross. Don't look back."

"You know how Abraham always talks about how he met Shadow? Well, it's a complete lie. Research Jackson Daniels when you get home, then let's meet up tomorrow evening around six."

"This sounds intriguing," she murmured.

"I don't have all the pieces but hopefully you'll be able to put this puzzle together. I don't know why they're lying about when they met, but I'm sure you'll get to the bottom of this."

"Lenni, please promise me that you'll leave this alone. Abraham is dangerous."

"Okay, I will, but I want to know how this all turns out."

"When it's over, I'll tell you everything," Phoenix said.

⌐⌐

BACK AT HOME, Lenni was a ball of nervousness as she paced across the hardwood floor of her living room. She had to confess her sins to her husband before Sophia had a chance to strike.

"Please let Eli forgive me, Lord," Lenni whispered. "He's a good man and he's been a good husband. He doesn't deserve this heartache..."

Lenni was about to go to the bedroom to shower and change when the doorbell sounded.

She opened the door. "What are you doing here?"

⌐⌐

JULIAN AND PHOENIX had just turned on the television when the news of Lenni's death came across the screen.

"Noooo…" she moaned. Tears overflowed and spilled down her face. She collapsed into his arms. "Whhhy…"

He held Phoenix close until she was all cried out.

She couldn't believe Lenni was dead. She'd just talked to her earlier that day and now she was gone. Phoenix didn't know what happened, but she knew that Abraham was connected to her friend's death.

She wiped her face with the back of her hands. "I can't believe this is happening. Eli must be devastated."

"They haven't mentioned a cause of death yet. Do you know if she was sick?"

"She wasn't," Phoenix responded.

She wanted to call Eli but decided against it. He was already dealing with a lot. He didn't need her being nosy.

"From the way they're talking, it almost sounds like it might have been a suicide," Julian said.

"That can't be true. Lenni would never do something like that. She wouldn't leave Eli this way."

"She may have been battling some demons you know nothing about. This is a lot even for you right now. Why don't you take a nice hot bath? I'll call later to check on you."

"Please don't leave," Phoenix said. "You can sleep in the other bedroom."

Julian nodded. "I'm not going anywhere if you want me to stay. I need to reach out to Eli to offer my condolences and see if there's anything I can do."

Chapter Thirty

"Eli said that he found her in the bathtub with her wrists slit," Abraham said when he hung up the phone the next morning. "Lenni killed herself."

"I hate to say it, but I'm not surprised," Sophia responded. "She's been acting a bit strange. I tried to get her to talk to me, but she refused."

Abraham shook his head in dismay. "I feel terrible for Eli. There aren't any right words for times like this."

Sophia opened the refrigerator and retrieved a carton of eggs. "You want scrambled or fried?"

He looked at her aghast. "Lenni's dead and you're thinking about food."

"I wasn't married to her and we weren't friends. I'm not going to pretend that I feel something I don't."

"I can't believe you sometimes," Abraham uttered in exasperation.

"You know she didn't like you either."

"None of that matters now. The woman is dead. She was

the wife of my associate pastor, Sophia. We have to show sympathy regardless of our true feelings."

"Only when we're out in public," she stated. "I'm in my house and I don't give a flip about Lenni Carpenter."

<hr />

PHOENIX WOULD NEVER EVER BELIEVE that Lenni committed suicide.

She stood in the front of her full-length mirror, eyeing the black dress she'd purchased just for this somber occasion.

When she walked out of her house, she found Julian standing near her car. He was dressed in a dark suit and carrying his Bible.

"I didn't know you were coming."

"I've always had a lot of respect for Eli, but I want to also be there for you. I know how hard these last few days have been."

"Thank you."

He kissed her. "Ready?"

"I think so."

"Let's take my car," Julian said.

On the drive to the church, he stole a peek at her and said, "You look like something's bothering you, Phoenix."

"Julian, I really don't believe Lenni committed suicide. She wanted to tell me something. This may sound crazy to you, but I think she was murdered to keep her from talking."

"By who?"

"I don't know. My instincts are telling me that this doesn't feel right to me."

"Are you one of those amateur detectives?" Julian asked, a grin on his face.

"I'm serious," Phoenix responded. "Lenni didn't kill herself."

"It was ruled a suicide. Eli found her in the tub. She'd slit her wrists, Phoenix."

"Julian, she wouldn't have done that."

"So, let's say you're right. Who do you think did this and why?" he asked.

"I think Abraham is responsible. I'm not saying he actually did it, but he's connected."

Julian's eyes grew wide in his surprise. "Why would you say that?"

"Lenni knew something about him and Shadow—something she was going to share with me. There's a lot you don't know about Abraham."

"But you do?"

"I've heard a lot of things and I read about him on the Internet. I know what happened when they were in Dallas."

"None of it makes the man a murderer, baby."

"There are a lot of pieces to this puzzle," Phoenix said. "I'm going to figure it out. I've got to do this."

━━━

INSTEAD OF ATTENDING THE REPAST, they returned to her townhome instead of attending the repast.

"Julian, I need to show you something." She pulled out a photograph and handed it to him.

"Who's this?" Julian asked.

"It used to be me."

He looked confused. "I don't understand."

"I had a terrible car accident and had to have facial reconstruction. It's been about three years now."

"Baby, I'm sorry."

"I believe that Abraham McCormick is behind what happened to me. I came to North Carolina to prove it. I want him to pay for all the dirt he's done and gotten away with."

"Phoenix, I understand that you're angry and you want justice. I get that, but you have to realize that while revenge may provide a lift, you could end up feeling worse. Besides, why are you so sure he did this?"

"Julian, people used to tell me how I looked like my mother. He stole that from me."

"Was there an investigation?"

"Yes, but he conveniently came up with a solid alibi."

"Baby, you really should leave this to the authorities."

"They're not doing anything, Julian. They can't seem to find any evidence strong enough to hold him. All I'm trying to do is prove that he's a monster."

"No, there's more to it. You want revenge."

Armed folded across her chest, Phoenix asked, "And you wouldn't, Julian?"

"Look, I know that thoughts of revenge are a basic human response, but you shouldn't act on them. Baby, the Bible says that we should overcome evil with good. We have to resist the impulse to retaliate. You know there is a key verse in God's Word which is found in the Old Testament and it's also quoted twice in the New Testament. It says, *do not take revenge, my dear friends, but leave room for God's wrath, for it is written: It is mine to avenge; I will repay.* It's not our right to usurp God's authority. We have to let him judge and pour out retribution as He sees fit, Phoenix."

"I hear what you're saying, Julian. But it seems that people like Abraham often get away with their crimes. I know the Bible tells us to love our enemies, but I can't. I just can't." A lone tear ran down her cheek. "But what hurts most is that Lenni is dead and I feel like it's my fault."

Julian pulled her into his embrace. "I'm so sorry, baby. What happened to Lenni is tragic, but it has nothing to do with you."

"I think it has everything to do with me."

Chapter Thirty-One

Fallon was seated on the sofa reading a book on pregnancy when Abraham arrived.

"You seem tense," she said, closing her book and laying it down on the coffee table. "What's going on with you?"

Abraham sat down beside her on the sofa. "I'm sure you heard that Eli lost his wife."

"Yeah, I did hear about that. I feel so bad for him. I didn't know Lenni very well, but when I worked at Holy Cross, she was really nice to me."

Abraham nodded. "She didn't care much for me, but she never let her personal feelings interfere with whatever we had to do when it came to the church. I still can't believe she took her own life."

Fallon gasped. "Did she leave a letter?"

"Not that I know of. Why?"

"She didn't seem like the type to do something so final and drastic."

"I thought so, too, but I guess none of us really knew her as well as we all thought."

She snuggled against him. "I think a lil' loving will take your mind off this, at least for a lil' while."

Abraham buried his face in her breasts. "I need you. I want you."

Fallon smiled. "I'm all yours."

<hr>

"WHAT'S WRONG, *UWETSI AGEYV?*"

"Dad, a woman I worked with at Holy Cross passed away. The coroner said it was suicide, but it doesn't fit her personality. Lenni never would've done this."

"You think she was murdered?"

"I do," Phoenix said.

"Do you think Abraham McCormick had anything to do with her death?"

"I don't know why he'd want to hurt her. Dad, I honestly don't know what to think. None of this makes sense."

"Maybe you didn't know her as well as you'd like to think."

"You might be right. It's just that on the day this happened, we were supposed to meet up. There was something she wanted to tell me, but she never got the chance."

"What do you think it was about?"

"I have no idea," she murmured, "but I'm going to get to the truth of what happened to Lenni."

Chapter Thirty-Two

Phoenix joined Julian on a day trip to Wilmington Beach.

She could feel his gaze on her. "Why are you staring at me?"

"I was trying to decide if you looked more like a Cynthia or a Phoenix."

"And?"

"You're definitely a Phoenix. I know that you think I don't understand what you're going through, but I do."

Phoenix turned in her chair to look at him. "How?"

"About six years ago, my brother was shot. He was on his way home when his car got a flat tire. This racist dude approached and started harassing my brother. He pulls out a gun and shots him."

Her heart broke for him. She couldn't imagine how it felt to lose a sibling. "Julian, I'm sorry."

"When I tell you that I truly had to decide between worldly and kingdom justice—that was a hard call. When the man who murdered my brother got twenty years in prison, I wasn't satisfied. I wanted him to serve a lifetime. I prepared a statement to read before the court at his sentencing. I felt like they needed to put him under the jail. But when it was my turn to speak. I looked him dead in the eyes—I wanted him to see my hatred for him. How I despised him for what he'd done to my brother. I wanted him to see how I wanted to avenge my brother's death."

"What happened?"

"God spoke in my heart and told me that I had to show this man compassion. That I had to forgive him." Julian's eyes filled with tears. "*Forgive* the man who took my brother from me. I was in ministry and those were the words I spoke to everyone dealing with unforgiveness. I could tell others but, in this instance,—I just wanted to rebel against God." He wiped at his eyes.

"I looked that dude in his eyes and told him that I forgave him. Suddenly, I was filled with compassion for him. I asked the Judge if I could pray with him."

"Wow…" Phoenix murmured.

"While I prayed, this man held my hand so tight and he cried like a baby. It was in that moment that I realized he truly regretted his actions."

"Julian, you are an amazing man. Right now, I'm so in awe of you. You truly live what you preach about."

"I still get in my flesh, Phoenix. I'm human, but I strive to be a better person each day."

"That's interesting that you mention that. Abraham has said that to me a couple of times."

"We are not sinless. It's a daily struggle to die to self. Like Abraham, I face constant battles, but I've learned to avoid temptation whenever possible."

"The guy who shot your brother. Is he still in prison?"

Julian nodded. "I see him once a month."

Phoenix was stunned. "You actually visit the man who killed your brother?"

"We do Bible study. He repented and gave his life to the Lord."

"I'm speechless."

"How could I continue to minister God's Word to my members if I'm unwilling to follow what it says?"

―――――

"YOU NEED to get out of here," Fallon stated. "Abraham will be pulling up any minute."

He brushed past her and into the apartment.

"You really think you have a chance with this man, don't you?"

"He intends to tell his wife about us. That we're having a baby, so yes. I'd say I have a good chance with him," Fallon said. "Look, I don't know what happened between you two, but all you need to do is talk to him. He's a really nice guy."

"I know him much better than you do—the real Abraham."

"I told you before that I want out. I'm not interested in destroying him or anyone—I have my child to think about."

"Fallon, it's not that simple. You know too much."

"I haven't said anything, and I won't. I promise. I can convince Abraham to leave town—even leave the country."

He laughed.

"You're not as bright as I thought you were. That man is not going to leave his wife for you."

"You're wrong," Fallon stated.

"He won't leave her because I'm not going to let him."

"What are you talking about?"

"I have a plan in place and I'm not about to let your feelings for Abraham interfere. I don't understand why you were stupid enough to let yourself get pregnant. It was supposed to be a lie, Fallon."

"I didn't get pregnant on purpose. It just happened."

"All the more convincing, I guess."

"You need to leave before Abraham gets here."

"I'll be long gone by the time he arrives. Unfortunately, so will you."

ABRAHAM ENTERED the apartment with two shopping bags stuffed with baby clothing and stuffed animals to find Fallon asleep on the sofa.

He sat the bags down and gave her a light nudge. "Wake up, sweetheart."

Abraham nudged her again. "C'mon… I have some things I want to show you."

Leaning closer to her face, realization dawned. Fallon wasn't breathing. He picked up her phone and dialed 9-1-1, then hung up.

I can't be caught here in this house with her.

Abraham grabbed the shopping bags and rushed back to his car. His whole body trembled in fear as he realized what this could mean to his career and his marriage.

He had to get home to Sophia.

But first, he had to get rid of the baby items.

Abraham stopped at the first daycare he found under the guise of making a donation.

"What's wrong?" Sophia asked when he burst through the

front door like an angry wind. "You look like you've seen a ghost."

"She's dead," he said pacing. "I can't believe this…"

"Who?"

"Fallon."

"Abraham, what did you do?"

He stopped in his tracks. "I didn't do anything, Sophia. I… I went to her place and found her dead."

"Did you touch anything?"

"No, but my fingerprints are all over the apartment." Abraham began to pace once again. "What if someone saw me leaving there. What if they recognized my car?"

He was visibly shaken.

"Calm down. We can have Shadow take care of this situation. You know you can trust him."

Chapter Thirty-Three

The next day when Phoenix got to work, everyone was talking about Fallon's death. The consensus was that she'd been murdered.

News reports were vague, which didn't surprise Phoenix. She knew the police would not release all of the details if they suspected foul play.

"We've had too much death lately," Olympia said when she came by the office to pick up a reimbursement check.

Phoenix agreed. "Did you know Fallon well?"

"Not really. For the most part, she kept pretty much to herself for the short time she worked here. You were her replacement, you know."

Lowering her voice, she whispered, "Lady Sophia couldn't stand Fallon. That's why she had Pastor McCormick fire her."

"I had no idea," Phoenix lied.

"It's such a shame she's gone."

Shadow walked in with so much as a knock. "I need to pick up Bobby's check. He's out with the flu."

"Here you go," she said. "Bobby called this morning."

"Thanks."

"That man makes me nervous," Olympia confided when Shadow left.

"Why?" Phoenix inquired.

"I don't know. I just don't like the way he lurks around here. He hardly says a word to anyone other than Pastor or Lady Sophia."

"He and the McCormick's have known each other a long time, haven't they?"

"No... where did you get an idea like that? Olympia said.

"I thought I'd heard that he worked for them when they were in Dallas."

"He did, but only for about a year before they moved here. Lady Sophia told me that Abraham met him at a men's conference. Apparently, there was an attempted robbery and Shadow intervened. Abraham was impressed with the way Shadow handled the situation. He hired him on the spot."

"Oh, so they didn't know him before then?"

"No," Olympia responded. "Honestly, I just wish they'd left him in Dallas."

Phoenix met her gaze. "He looks intimidating, but he's security. He's just doing his job."

"I suppose you're right."

"Olympia, could you please let Pastor McCormick know that I'm leaving for the day? I'm not feeling the best and I don't want to make anyone else sick."

"Oh yes, you should go home. I know I don't want to catch anything. I'll spray your office down with Lysol. You go on and get out of here."

Phoenix gave a fake cough. "Thank you."

She felt just fine, but Phoenix wanted to do some

researching of her own on Shadow and his relationship with Abraham.

It was time for some answers.

It was time for the truth to come out about everything.

———

PHOENIX KNEW that Shadow had been in the military before he worked for the FBI. *Why would you leave a job like that to come work with Abraham? Maybe he just wasn't interested in working in law enforcement.* Deep down, Phoenix felt like there was much more to that story. She made a couple of calls to former contacts.

"Where have you been, Cynthia? It's like you just disappeared?"

"Katherine, I'm working an assignment. I can't go into the details, but I need your help."

"I'll do what I can..."

———

ABRAHAM KNEW SOONER or later the police would show up at his door. Wanting to avoid any hint of scandal at the church, he called the station and arranged for them to meet at his home. He'd tried to persuade Sophia to go to the church, but she insisted on remaining by his side.

"The police are here," Sophia told Abraham. "I can't believe we're going through this again."

They settled in the living room.

"When the detectives looked at Sophia, she said, "I'm not going anywhere. This is my home."

"We can discuss anything in front of her."

"Okay," the female detective said. "We found a photograph of you and Miss Sutherland in her apartment. What was the nature of your relationship?"

Abraham glanced up at Sophia's stoic expression, then responded, "We... we were involved."

"I knew about their relationship."

"How long have you known?"

"From the beginning," Sophia said. "I'm sure this will probably shock you, but Abraham and I have an understanding when it comes to other women."

"Were you still involved with her at the time of her death?"

"Yes, I was."

The detectives exchanged looks.

"Were you aware that Miss Sutherland was pregnant?"

Sophia gasped. "Abraham..."

He nodded. "I knew about the baby. As you can see, I hadn't had a chance to disclose this to my wife."

Sophia crossed the floor in quick strides.

"This is particularly upsetting to her because we've tried for years to conceive."

"Where were you on the day Miss Sutherland died?" the male detective inquired.

"I was shopping for the baby." Abraham opened his wallet and pulled out a receipt. "I donated them to a daycare."

"Witnesses identified you as being at her apartment on that day."

"I wanted to surprise Fallon with the gifts, but when I got there and realized she was dead, I panicked. I called 9-1-1, then hung up and left. I was trying to get home to Sophia."

"Why is that?"

"Because she's my wife and I wanted to make sure she was okay. There have been threats against my life. Someone killed

Fallon—I believe it was to hurt me. I'm sure you've done your background checks on me. You know that I've been accused of drugging and raping women—I was cleared of those charges. However, there's someone out there who thinks I'm guilty. I was shot in my arm—we left Dallas because we thought we were in danger."

"Seems like danger follows you around," the female detective commented.

"I never would've hurt Fallon. She was carrying my child." A lone tear fell from his eye.

"That was my only chance to be a father."

Chapter Thirty-Four

Phoenix stared at the computer screen in disbelief.

Abraham was a manipulating liar. He and Shadow apparently had a long history together. She printed out the photograph, placing it in the folder along with the other information she'd gathered over the years during her investigation of McCormick since the beginning.

"Something's not adding up," she whispered as she went over dates and back through her notes, including her interviews with each of the women, including Nadine.

Determined, Phoenix ran a search on military records. The more information she found, led to other leads.

Three hours later, her friend emailed over an essential document that would connect all of the pieces together.

It was time to confront Abraham with what she knew.

◁▭▷

FALLON WAS pregnant and Abraham had kept it from her.

He was having a baby with another woman. Tears escaped Sophia's eyes and rolled down her cheeks.

She used the spare key to let herself into Shadow's place and waited for him to arrive.

"I saw a police car in your driveway."

Sophia wiped her face. "They're questioning him about his relationship with Fallon."

"How did they find out?"

"They found a photograph of the two of them together. I'm sure they also found his fingerprints and DNA in the apartment—I guess you weren't as thorough as you thought. It wasn't hard to put two and two together."

"Sophia, are you okay?"

She shook her head no. "Did you know that Fallon was pregnant? Please tell me that you wouldn't keep something like this from me. You know how I feel about my infertility."

"That's not something Abraham would tell me. I'm not his confidante—I'm just the head of his security team."

"So, you're saying that you didn't know?" Sophia asked.

"I didn't know anything about the baby." After a brief pause, he asked, "What will you do now?"

Sophia picked up her purse. "Wait until he leaves the house to go home. I can't stand being anywhere near Abraham right now."

━━━

WHEN THE DETECTIVES were done with the interview, Abraham searched the house for Sophia. When he couldn't find her, he drove to the church.

In his office, he sat in his chair staring out the window, unable to concentrate on his work. *I never wanted Sophia to find out like this. It had only taken one look at my face and she knew. She knew that I was going to leave her to be with Fallon. I have to find a way to make her understand that this was never about love but a sense of duty to my child. I will always love her.*

Abraham pulled out his phone to call his wife.

No answer.

He hadn't really expected her to pick up. Sophia was angry but more than that—she was hurt.

Abraham stayed in his office until everyone had gone home. He could see his dreams slowly evaporating away. He knew it was only a matter of time when the news of his relationship with Fallon would surface in light of this investigation.

All the good I've done won't matter.

He thought about the apartments where he grew up—now empty and rundown. The housing development even in its day, was nothing to brag about, but it was his first and only real home. His parents didn't have much money, but their hearts overflowed with love. Abraham wanted to honor them by revitalizing the apartments to provide housing for the homeless. He wanted to offer onsite career training and other programs to help them get back on track with life, but mostly to keep families together.

"Heavenly Father, I confess I'm a sinner—an adulterer. I'm not worthy of Your love; yet I know You love me unconditionally. I know that You judge the heart of men. You know that I have a heart for You. I am sick of the way I've been living. I've hurt so many people. I ask your forgiveness, Father. I—"

Abraham stopped short when he heard a noise. He wasn't alone in the building. He got up and rushed out into the hallway. "Sophia... sweetheart is that you?"

Chapter Thirty-Five

"You want me to do what?" Julian asked.

"Come with me to Holy Cross…" Phoenix took him by the hand, leading him over to the sofa. When they were seated, she said, "I have to tell you something."

"What is it?"

"I need to go see Abraham. I've found out some stuff and I have to talk to him. It's fine if you don't want to get involved. I just didn't want to go alone but I will if I have to," she told him. "I have to talk to him tonight."

"Is this all you're going to tell me?"

"For now," Phoenix responded. "I need you to trust me."

"I hope I don't come to regret this," Julian said.

"You won't. I promise."

SOPHIA TURNED to find Abraham standing in the doorway

of the bathroom. She adjusted the belt on her robe. "I want you out of this house tonight," she uttered, brushing past him.

"C'mon love…"

His sudden laugher made her skin crawl.

"Stop acting like you're suddenly a saint in this marriage."

Her first thought was that he'd been drinking because he wasn't acting like himself.

Sophia needed a glass of wine to calm her nerves.

She heard the front door open and close. Sophia peeked around the corner, hoping Abraham had decided to heed her words and leave.

When she realized it was Shadow, she said, "I'm glad you're here. Abraham's been drinking and I want him out of this house tonight."

"I came by to make sure you're okay," he responded.

"I'd be much better if my whore of a husband wasn't here. I told him to leave. Maybe you should go upstairs and help him pack."

"Sophia there's something you need to know. The man upstairs… that's not Abraham."

She was thoroughly confused. "What are you talking about?"

Keeping his voice low, Shadow said, "I need you to leave with me right now, Sophia. I'll explain everything to you later." He grabbed her gently. "We need to get out of here."

She snatched her arm away. "I'm not going anywhere. I'm not dressed and besides, this is my house. I'm not the one leaving. I'm not the one who violated our agreement."

"You heard my *wife*. She doesn't want to go anywhere with you."

Sophia turned around to face the man standing near the

stairs. Her gaze traveled slowly from his face to his shoes then upward. "Dear Lord..." she whispered. "W-who are you?"

"I'm your beloved husband. Who else would I be?"

She shook her head. "No, you're not Abraham. Where is my husband?"

"Where he belongs... burning in hell."

"Jacob..." Shadow interjected. "Leave Sophia out of this."

"You know *him*?" she asked. "You knew all along that Abraham had a twin brother and you never thought to mention it to me? How could you do this?" She sent a sharp glare in his direction before returning her attention to Jacob. "What do you want?"

"I want everything," he responded. "The house... the money... everything that should have been mine in the first place."

"Abraham and I worked for everything we have," Sophia stated. "Where do you come off thinking you can just walk in and take it?"

He laughed. "See you think you know what's going on, but you don't have a clue."

Sophia folded her arms across her chest. "I'm sure you're going to enlighten me."

"Did you know your husband was adopted?"

"No. He never told me."

"The people who adopted Abraham chose me—I was the one they wanted. They couldn't afford to take both of us, so they worked out a private adoption with our aunt. They would raise me while she kept Abraham. They promised that my brother and I would be able to spend time together—just wouldn't grow up in the same household. The day they came to get me... Abraham wanted to play a game or so he led me to believe. He locked me inside of a closet in the basement. He was gone by the time my aunt found me."

"I don't believe you," Sophia uttered. "Abraham wouldn't do anything like that."

"He stole the family that was supposed to be mine. He robbed me of a normal childhood—a life without all the hell I went through."

"I'm sorry, but you have to know that Abraham was just a child trying to survive."

"So was I. We shared a womb and he turned his back on me."

"Well, it sounds like you didn't have a problem leaving him behind," she pointed out.

"*They chose me.*"

Sophia eyed Shadow. "What's your part in all this?"

"Jacob and I were in the military together. He saved my life. I promised to help him reclaim his birthright."

"So, you manipulated us."

"I helped my friend," Shadow responded. "I owed him."

"You also owe me your loyalty," Sophia responded. "I actually believed you when you said you cared for me." She shook her head in dismay. "I am such a fool."

"I meant it when I said I love you."

Jacob burst into laughter. "Man… what's wrong with you. I told you not to get involved with this woman. She and my brother deserve each other. I told you she didn't care nothing for you. That's how women are—they play with your emotions."

Sophia glared at Jacob. "Shadow, I do care for you. Don't listen to him."

"Then leave with me right now."

"I can't. Don't get me wrong… I don't intend to stay with

Abraham, but I'm not going to just walk away from everything I've help him build." She looked over at Jacob. "I'm not letting you take it from me either."

"The dead don't need money or fancy mansions."

Sophia shivered.

"I told you to leave her out of this."

"My *wife* and I will settle in the living room while you go clean out the safe."

Shadow looked reluctant to leave Sophia.

"She'll be fine as long as she behaves," Jacob assured him. "You won't disappoint me, will you?"

PHOENIX WALKED BRISKLY DOWN the hallway leading to Abraham's office the folder and photograph clenched in her hand.

She could see that his door was slightly ajar and released a sigh of relief. He was here working late.

Fear crept in as she neared, noting the smoke swirling in the air and smelled fumes. Something was on fire.

Phoenix took a deep breath and eased inside, nearly stumbling over what felt like a body inside. She turned on the flashlight on her phone. "Abraham…"

She knelt down beside him nudging him. "Abraham, what happened?"

He moaned.

Phoenix sagged with relief. "Thank the Lord," she whispered. "We need to get you out of here. C'mon Abraham."

A groan of anguish was his response."

"There's a fire in your office. We need to get out of here,"

Phoenix stated. She helped him to his feet. "You're bleeding. What happened?"

"Someone knocked me out." He released a low groan as he tried to sit up. "I've... I've been getting threatening letters." He touched his head gingerly. "Someone is really out to take me out."

"I have a feeling I know who it was," she stated.

"Who?"

"Your brother."

Abraham frowned. "Jacob?" Shaking his head, he continued, "Phoenix, that can't be. My brother died years ago."

"He's very much alive."

Abraham stopped in his tracks. "How do you know this?"

"It's a long story. I have a feeling your wife's in danger," Phoenix said. "Let's get out of here. We can call the police on the way to your house. The fire department should be here at any moment."

When she and Abraham walked out of the building, they were met by Julian who asked, "What happened?"

"I found him on the floor," Phoenix explained. "He was unconscious. Someone knocked him out. Someone started a fire in his office."

Julian examined Abraham's head. "He needs to go to the hospital."

"No, I need to get to my wife. Sophia may be in danger."

"What in the world is going on?" Julian wanted to know.

"Can you wait here for the fire department?" Phoenix asked. "I need to get Abraham to his wife. I promise I'll explain everything when this is over."

"I'm going to hold you to it."

Chapter Thirty-Six

"You stay here and wait for the police," Abraham said when she parked her car two houses down. This is between Jacob and me. I don't want anybody else to get hurt."

"You're in no condition for a confrontation," Phoenix countered. "Let me come inside with you."

"I'll be fine. I just need to talk to my brother." He looked at her. "Enough people have been hurt."

He made his way to the door and entered the house.

Abraham found Jacob pacing and Sophia seated on the sofa. He'd never seen her look so scared.

"Jacob…" Abraham said. "This is between you and me."

"I didn't expect to see you so soon. I thought I'd knocked you out pretty good."

When Shadow strode into the room, Abraham glared at him. "You were supposed to protect my wife."

"Protect her," his brother uttered. "He's her lover."

Stunned, Abraham eyed his wife. "Sophia…"

"Why didn't you tell me you were a twin?" She asked. "Or the fact that you were adopted. I've been asking you for years to tell me everything. I bet you told Fallon though. Why is that?"

Abraham ignored her questions. He would explain everything later if they survived his brother's tirade. "Jacob, I thought you were dead. I was told that you'd died."

"You left me in that basement and stole the family I was supposed to have."

"I was wrong for that, Jacob. I couldn't live with what I'd done to you, so I told them the truth. How I desperately wanted a family, and how much I missed you. I asked them to take me back to Aunt Mag's house. I was going to straighten everything out, but when we got there—we were told that you and Aunt Mag died in a car accident."

Jacob muttered a string of curses. "Stop lying. Aunt Mag couldn't afford to keep both of us and those people said they could only care for one child."

"They changed their minds. I'm telling you the truth," Abraham stated. "They were going to raise us together."

"Aunt Mag's bum of a boyfriend started beating on her, and when I would try to protect her, he would beat me. Then he…" Jacob shook his head. "*She* died that night trying to escape from that beast. I ran away from the accident but ended up in a group home for boys. One that pimped us out for sex to the highest bidder."

"I had no idea…"

"Of course, you wouldn't," Jacob uttered. "You lived a perfect life with the family that was supposed to be mine." He glared at his twin. "I should've killed you instead of just shooting you in the arm."

"It was *you* that night? Tell me why?" Abraham insisted. "Do you hate me this much?"

"More than you can ever imagine." Pulling out a gun, he said, "The only reason you're still alive is because I intend to see you go to prison for your girl's murder and that woman from your church."

"You mean Lenni? What does she have to do with this?"

"She saw me at Hammond's. I couldn't risk her saying anything so I shut her up."

Bristling, Abraham said, "Fallon was carrying my child when you killed her."

"I knew she was pregnant. Heck, I'm the reason you met her in the first place. I paid her to be your lover," Jacob said. "It was my plan all along for her to work in the accounting office. She was supposed to transfer money into my account every week, but then you fired her, so we had to come up with another plan."

"What do you intend to do with us now?" Abraham asked.

"I haven't quite decided. There are too many loose ends and I don't intend on going to prison."

"Jacob, you're not going to be able to get away with this."

PHOENIX COULDN'T JUST SIT out in the car not knowing what was happening inside.

She crept around the house. Phoenix found the patio door unlocked and eased inside, following the voices until she could see Abraham clearly. They were all gathered in the formal living room. She stood outside in the foyer listening.

"Brother, I have to tell you—you've got to be the luckiest man in the world. I figured you'd be the main suspect in that reporter's accident, but like the rape—you conveniently had an alibi. I won't make that mistake a third time."

"You ran Cynthia Highcloud off the road?"

"Yep," Jacob boasted. "The plan was for the police to believe you had motive and were the one responsible. I knew everyone would blame you because she exposed you as a rapist."

"Please put the gun away," Sophia pleaded. "Jacob, we're sorry about all the bad things that happened to you. Abraham and I will write you a check for $100,000 dollars. It won't erase what happened but at least you can start over somewhere."

"I'll get money and more before this is all over," Jacob responded. "You should've taken Shadow up on his offer. Now you both get to die. Now that I think about it… once I get rid of Abraham's body; I can step up and be the grieving widower."

"You're not gonna touch Sophia," Shadow stated.

"Man, didn't you hear what she's been saying? Her only concern is for Abraham. *She don't want you.*"

"I didn't sign on for murder." He took a step toward Jacob. "That wasn't part of the plan. Let's just get this money and get out of here."

"If you'd done your job the right way, Abraham would've been in jail for rape already."

"I suppose it's my fault the reporter lived, too."

Jacob shook his head. "Naw, that was on me. I really didn't think she'd make it."

"Let's just get out of here," Shadow stated.

Jacob shook his head. "No, I'm here to reclaim what's mine."

"I don't have a good feeling about this."

Phoenix's eyes traveled her surroundings, looking for a

place to hide should it become necessary. The police should be arriving any minute, she thought. *What's taking them so long? They should've been here by now.*

Phoenix heard movement and backed away from the doorway, accidentally knocking over the vase that was on the table in the foyer.

In an instance, she was staring into the eyes of the man who'd tried to kill her that night.

"What do we have here?" Jacob asked, gesturing for Phoenix to join them in the living room.

"What is she doing here?" Sophia asked.

"I asked Phoenix to come by to pick up some paperwork," Abraham lied.

"That's too bad," his brother uttered. "How long have you been standing out there?"

"Not long," she said. Phoenix stared at Jacob. "I have no wish to be involved with your family drama."

"Then you've come to the wrong place."

"Obviously," she responded.

"Where's your phone?" Shadow asked.

"It's in my car. I just came to do a quick pick up as Abraham said. I didn't think I'd need it since my intent was to run in and out."

"See if she's telling the truth," Jacob said.

Shadow patted her down. "No phone."

Abraham had cautioned her to stay in the car but she became restless and didn't listen. Now she wished she'd done so.

Phoenix caught flashes of red and blue in her peripheral view and released a soft sigh. She hoped Jacob and Shadow hadn't noticed.

Her gaze met Sophia's. She knew the police were outside

from the expression on her face.

Abraham took a step toward Jacob. "I'm begging you to let Sophia and Phoenix go. They don't have anything to do with this."

"The plan's blown," Shadow interjected. "Unless you want to spend the rest of your life in prison—we need to disappear. My debt to you is paid, Jacob."

"It's paid when I say so."

"I'm not doing this with you." Shadow walked over to the window. "I told you… the cops…"

The front door blew open with the force of several police officers, guns cocked and ready to shoot.

Muttering a string of curses, Jacob dropped his weapon. "This isn't over," he told Abraham.

⊏⊐

"I DON'T KNOW how I can ever repay you for what you did," Abraham said. "If you hadn't come by the church earlier… I don't know what would've happened." He paused. "By the way… why were you there?"

"To tell you about Shadow," Phoenix responded, "and about your brother."

"How did you find out about Jacob?"

"Perhaps I should start at the beginning. I'm Cynthia Highcloud version 2."

Abraham eyed her in disbelief. "Cynthia…" Clearing his throat, he said, "You came here under a false identity? To do what? Prove my guilt?"

"I wasn't going to let you get away with attacking another woman. Nadine was my friend. I didn't want you to get away. But now I realized that I was wrong. It wasn't you who raped those women. I guess I owe you an apology. I'm sorry."

"Has your opinion of me truly changed?" he asked.

"I honestly don't know what to think," Phoenix responded. "You manipulate people's faith and it's not right. But the plans you have for revitalizing your old neighborhood is admirable. Regardless of what I think of your infidelities, the Anointed Water and all that—I judged you unfairly."

"After meeting Jacob, I can understand why you thought it was me." Abraham shook his head. "We're identical. It just never occurred to me that he was still alive or that he was close by."

"It's uncanny," Sophia said as she walked toward them. "I knew that something was up with you, Phoenix… Cynthia… whoever you are. So, what happens now? You leave and never bother us again? Because that would work for me."

"Sophia the feeling is mutual." Phoenix glanced over at Abraham, asking, "What will you do now?"

"I'm stepping down from the pulpit. I'm not sure I ever belonged up there. I chose that path because others told me it was my calling. I can't say I heard this directive from the Lord."

"I think you're making the right decision. Maybe you are called to ministry—but not in the pulpit."

"Eli will take over as Senior Pastor. He's the perfect replacement for me. I'm going to continue working on my housing project—getting families off the street and into homes."

"How will you raise the money?"

"As you know, a lot of donations came in. I invested most of my salary and it's paid off. I'll also look into some grant funding. I can help a lot of people. After what just happened with Jacob, I want more than ever to keep families together."

———

LATER AFTER EVERYONE WAS GONE, Abraham found Sophia upstairs in the room that was supposed to be the nursery. She was sitting in the rocking chair clutching a teddy bear.

"How are you?" Abraham inquired.

"Was Jacob telling the truth?" Sophia asked. "Were you really going to leave me? After all the crap I put up with—the women… you were going to choose *her*."

"I couldn't abandon my child. I wanted to be in my child's life—don't you get it? I was going to choose the child. Not Fallon, but I knew you couldn't have handled that."

"I do get it, Abraham, but it still hurts."

"Were you in love with Shadow?"

Sophia shook her head. "No. He was just a way to pass the time and get back at you for your womanizing ways."

Abraham tenderly arranged the bedding in the crib. "He was in love with you. I saw the way he looked at you before they put him in that police car."

"He was playing us, Abraham. He and Jacob manipulated us every step of the way. Shadow didn't love me. It was just a game."

He released a short sigh. "It was the same with Fallon. Jacob paid her to be my lover. It was probably his plan all along for her to get pregnant. To be honest, I'm not sure it was my baby."

Sophia looked up at him. "The doctors always said your sperm count was too low. You may be right—even if you requested a DNA test… he's your twin. You have to admit that it was a perfect plan."

"But why kill her?"

"Because maybe she really did fall in love with you, Abraham. If that's the case, then she became a threat. Jacob feared that she'd tell you the truth, so she had to go."

"So, where do we go from here?" he asked.

"I don't know about you, but this is where I get off this train." She rose to her feet and walked over to him, meeting his gaze. "I love you, Abraham, but the one thing I've learned from this experience is that you and I want two different things. You truly want to save the world and I couldn't care less. I only want to survive by being rich." She placed the teddy bear at the head of the crib. "I'm leaving for Los Angeles in the morning. Maybe I'll have better luck out there."

"I want nothing but the best for you, Sophia. I hope you find what you're looking for and more."

She kissed him. "I wish the same for you, Abraham."

———

PHOENIX KNOCKED on Abraham's door, a few days later. He was inside boxing up his possessions.

"Please come in. I hadn't expected to see you."

"I wanted to let you know that Nadine and Adrienne are aware of everything that's happened. They know that it was Jacob who attacked them and not you. The station is also going to issue an official apology. Here is a copy of mine." She placed the document on the edge of his desk.

"Thank you. After everything you've been through—you didn't have to do this."

"All of this started because of my story," Phoenix said. "I

blamed you for my accident. I blamed you for everything honestly."

"Jacob set this in motion way before you ever got involved," Abraham stated.

"Have you talked to him?"

"I've tried. He refuses to see me." Abraham released a short sigh. "I'm not going to abandon him this time. My adoptive parents really did go back to persuade my aunt to let them adopt Jacob as well. We got there too late. If we hadn't... maybe he'd be a different person."

"Other cases have come to light, Abraham," Phoenix said. "Jacob is a serial rapist."

"I won't abandon him a second time. I'm going to see that my brother gets the help he needs."

"He's going to jail for a long time. I don't know if you know this, but he killed your aunt's boyfriend. Bashed his head in with a bat."

Tears filled Abraham's eyes.

"I'm sorry," Phoenix said. "But you have to know that you can't blame yourself for who your brother became. And you can't save everyone—no matter how much you may want to— some people just don't want to be saved."

"My actions set all of this in motion," he responded.

"It was hard for me to forgive the people who wronged me, Abraham, but I've learned that it's even harder at times to forgive yourself."

He nodded in agreement. "I don't know that I can ever forgive myself for the choices I made."

"I hope that you can," Phoenix said as she turned to leave. She paused in the doorway asking, "How is Sophia handling all this?"

"I don't know. She's moved to Los Angeles," Abraham

said. "We're getting a divorce. It's probably for the best. I wasn't a good husband, but I hope that one day—I will be much better if I'm fortunate enough to find a wife."

He met her gaze. "So, what are you going to do? Go back to being Cynthia Highcloud?"

Phoenix shook her head. "I'm no longer that person. I'm not sure what's next, but I'm really looking forward to the future. For the first time in a long while—I feel renewed and refreshed. I'm actually excited about this next journey."

"I wish you much success," Abraham said.

"Same here," she responded. "Don't take this the wrong way, but I really hope you stay out of the news and on television unless it's for a good cause. "

He chuckled. "Goodbye Phoenix."

Julian was standing outside the car when she walked outside of the administration building. "How did it go?"

"Great," she said with a smile.

He embraced her. "Are you ready for this?"

"Yes. I am going to walk into **WRAL** and snag that news anchor/reporter position."

"How do your parents feel about you legally changing your name to Phoenix?" Julian asked.

"They're fine with it," she responded.

"Just don't get too attached to D'Angelo," Julian said cryptically.

Phoenix looked at him and laughed. "C'mon, I want to get to my interview early so I can settle my nerves."

"I love you and I'm so proud of you."

She reached over and took his hand into her own. "I love you, too."

"The name Phoenix really does fit you," Julian said.

"Despite the flames that were designed to destroy you—you emerged transformed and more beautiful than ever."

"I was a reborn and given a new beginning. I'm not going to spend another moment rolling around in regrets, anger and unforgiveness. I'm ready to live my best life. I just hope you can keep up, Pastor Julian Nelson."

"Baby, I'm already ahead of you."

About the Author

Jacquelin Thomas is an award-winning, bestselling author with more than 80 titles in print and 23 years of experience as a published author. Her books have garnered several awards, including two EMMA awards, Romance in Color Reviewers Award, Readers' Choice Award, and the Atlanta Choice Award in the Religious & Spiritual category.

Jacquelin was a 2005 honoree at the Houston Black Film Festival for the movie adaptation of her novel, Hidden Blessings. She also received a Lifetime Achievement Award from Romantic Times Magazine.

Jacquelin is published in the romance, women's fiction, inspirational and young adult genres. Her second book in the young adult series, Divine Confidential was nominated for a 2008 NAACP Image Award for outstanding fiction.

Jacquelin holds undergraduate degrees in Interior Design, Business Management and Psychology. She also has an M.L.S. in Legal Studies, and a M.S. in Psychology.

Also by Jacquelin Thomas

Poison Pen

Legacy

Jezebel

Jezebel's Daughter

Jezebel's Revenge

Jezebel's Redemption

Jezebel: The Prequel

The Ideal Wife

Visit: www.jacquelin-thomas.com for complete book list